GRAY TIDE IN THE EAST
An alternate history of the First World War

Andrew J. Heller

GRAY TIDE IN THE EAST
An alternate history of the First World War

Introduction to this Edition

When *Gray Tide in the East* was originally published in 2013, it did not turn out to be the book I had envisioned when I started, and soon after it appeared, I wanted to make changes and additions. Three years have passed since then, and I think it is about time finally go ahead.

In this 2nd Edition I had the opportunity to correct errors in the original version pointed out by some of my sharp-eyed and knowledgeable readers, further explain certain matters that some readers found confusing, and add new textual material in the Afterwords, including coverage of the effects of the historical changes in World War One on the Ottoman Empire, and a new essay on military technology and the war.

However, I do not consider these changes sufficient reasons to justify a new edition. What I believe does justify it are the illustrations. I had collected numerous photographs of people, places and things described in *Gray Tide*, and these photographs were an integral part of the book as I had originally conceived it. For various reasons, they were not included in either the e-book version or the paperback as published. I am pleased to be able to present them here, so that what you hold in your hands is the Gray Tide in the East as I intended it to be. I look forward to your comments on this new edition.

Andrew Heller

Acknowledgement

I would like to acknowledge the tireless efforts of my wife Carol, who encouraged me to write this book, then took time from her overcrowded schedule to painstakingly proofread and edit it. Without her, there might have been a *Gray Tide in the East*, but it would have been a very different, and much inferior book. Any remaining mistakes were made by me, during one of my many revisions.

Foreword

On August 1, 1914 Germany struck the first blow of what would later be called the First World War by sending 750,000 troops flooding through the small neutral countries of Luxembourg and Belgium into northern France.   The invasion of Belgium had the immediate consequence of bringing the British Empire into the war against Germany, which would not have otherwise happened. The violation of Belgium therefore was the direct cause of the British blockade of Germany, which in turn led to the German counter-blockade by the use of unrestricted submarine warfare (meaning that the submarines would sink any vessel, British or neutral in the waters around the British Isles).   BY 1917, unrestricted submarine warfare proved to be the main reason the United States joined the coalition that finally defeated Germany in 1918, after more than 4 years of the bloodiest war in modern history.

The invasion of Belgium almost did not happen. Kaiser Wilhelm II, Emperor of Germany, had a shrewder political sense than his advisors and generals. Fearing the invasion would result in Great Britain's declaration of war against Germany and put Germany in the position of the aggressor in the opinion of the world, the Kaiser cancelled the invasion on his own authority, and urged his commanding general to scrap the entire war plan, suggesting that the troops be sent East instead, against France's ally, Russia. The Chief of the General Staff, General Helmuth von Moltke persuaded the Kaiser to withdraw his stop order, and the invasion went ahead as planned.

But what if things had gone a little differently that day between the General and the Kaiser…?

(All photographs in public domain. The author wishes to thank the Library of Congress, the Imperial War Museums, the United States Navy and the Deutsches Bundesarchiv)

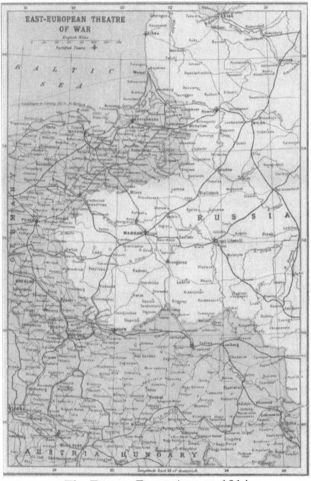

The Eastern Front, August, 1914

It is equal to living in a tragic land
To live in a tragic time.
Regard now the sloping, mountainous rocks
And the river that batters its way over stones,
Regard the hovels of those that live in this land.

It was the battering of drums I heard,
It was hunger, it was the hungry that cried
And the waves, the waves were soldiers moving,
Marching and marching in a tragic time
Below me, on the asphalt, under the trees.

It was soldiers went marching over the rocks,
And still the birds came, came in watery flocks,
Because it was spring, and the birds had to come.
No doubt that soldiers had to be marching,
And that drums had to be rolling, rolling, rolling.

Wallace Stevens
Dry Loaf

Chapter One: Berlin, August 1, 1914

General Helmuth Johann Ludwig von Moltke marched down the corridors of the Hohenzollern royal palace, looking neither to the left nor to the right. A Colonel followed, carrying his briefcase. One look at the General's face, with its deeply furrowed brow, its mouth that turned downward in a thin line and droopy gray mustache, would be sufficient for any reasonably impartial observer to conclude that here was a man who took a serious view of life. Nor would this same observer be surprised to learn that General von Moltke was known to his subordinates on the German Imperial General Staff (behind his back, naturally) as *der traurige Julius*, which might be rendered into English as "Gloomy Gus". In truth, the Chief of the General Staff was a pessimist by nature, and the day's events had done nothing to brighten his outlook.

Moltke had only this morning issued the orders that would set the Imperial war machine into motion, sending the right wing of the German Army sweeping across the fields of Belgium and on into northern France, beginning the march of three-quarters of a million men that would land a knockout punch on the left flank of the unsuspecting French Army.

In a few hours, elements of the 16th Division of the Fourth Army were scheduled to cross the border of Luxembourg to serve as the hinge for the main movement of the First, Second and Third Armies farther to the north. These three armies would deliver the key blow to the flank and rear of the French Army, a maneuver that would, if all went as planned, win the war in six weeks, in a single titanic battle of annihilation.

The movements of the Imperial Army had been calculated on a precise schedule, but suddenly a wrench had been thrown into the gears at the worst possible moment, by Kaiser Wilhelm II. The Emperor had halted the invasion, completely bypassing the Table of Organization and disregarding the General Staff by sending an order directly to the commander of the 16th Division, ordering him to stop until he received an order to proceed from the Kaiser himself. He had then summoned Moltke to the palace, no doubt to explain this new brainstorm, the latest and worst timed instance of Imperial meddling in military affairs.

The operational plan for the invasion of Belgium had not originated with Moltke. He had inherited it from his predecessor, Count Alfred von Schlieffen. Schlieffen developed his plan in 1905, after the Russo-Japanese War had exposed some of the glaring deficiencies in the corrupt and ineffectual Czarist military establishment. Schleiffen's approach was designed to take advantage of the Russian weaknesses revealed during the fighting against the Japanese in Siberia, particularly their slow rate of mobilization and poor logistics.

By 1905, the opposing military alliance systems of the Triple Alliance of Germany, Austria-Hungary and Italy against the Dual Entente of France and Russia had been in place for a decade. Ever since, all of these Great Powers had steadily built their armies and navies in preparation for a future great war, although no one knew when the next war would come, nor why.

Under these circumstances, it was not surprising that the German General Staff had assumed that whenever the war finally did start, it would be fought on two fronts: against France in the West, and Russia in the East, foes who presented very different strengths and weaknesses.

Modern, industrialized France was a reasonably compact nation, with an extensive railroad system, a good road network and an efficient military organization. She could be counted on to mobilize her army quickly - as quickly as Germany, in fact.

Russia, on the other hand, was an enormous, sprawling country, with fewer miles of railway than her ally (and far fewer in proportion to the area served), primitive roads, and a notoriously corrupt and incompetent military establishment. The Russian Army, moreover, had been thoroughly humiliated by the Japanese in the Russo-Japanese War in 1904-05. For these reasons, German war planners calculated that the Russians would be at least eight weeks behind both Germany and France in mobilizing their forces after the war broke out.

The military geography of the East and West provided another stark contrast. Germany's border with France stretched from the thickly forested and nearly roadless Ardennes in the north, through the rugged Vosges Mountains down to the Swiss border. This terrain was unsuitable for the rapid movement of large armies, and the border was protected by a series of fortresses on the French side from Verdun to Belfort, fortifications built for the express purpose of meeting and repelling a German invasion. In this country, defenders would have all the advantages and attackers none. Progress there would be measured in meters rather than kilometers and the meters would be purchased with blood. Schlieffen, like his predecessors, concluded that attacking here would be folly, and he refused to consider it.

In the East, however, the rolling farm country of Russian Poland and the Ukraine offered plenty of scope for maneuvering great masses of men, and even more for utilizing Germany's greatest military asset: its Krupp artillery, the finest in the world. Moreover, with such a vast country to attack, it would be relatively easy for the invaders to find weak points to break through the Russian lines, as they could not be strong everywhere, especially if they were as slow to mobilize their forces as expected.

Therefore, the obvious thing to do was to take advantage of Russia's presumed inability to mobilize quickly, by sending the bulk of the mobile striking forces East, to knock the Czar's huge but disorganized armies (the so-called "Russian steamroller") out of the war before they could become effective, or at least dislocate her mobilization. Indeed, this had been the basis for the German war plans as prepared by the Imperial General Staff before 1905, when Schlieffen was appointed.

The new Chief rejected this approach. Russia might be slow, its army inefficient and its General Staff incompetent, but there were two factors that weighed against the possibility of a quick decision in the East.

One was the sheer size of the opponent. There were just too many kilometers of Russia, endless kilometers over which an invading army's supplies had to be hauled by mule-drawn wagons on abysmal roads (where there were any roads at all), or over the inadequate rail network. As invaders had discovered over the centuries, campaigning in Russia was all too likely to become a logistical nightmare.

The second factor was the presence of the Russian General who had defeated some of the greatest military geniuses in European history, including Charles XII of Sweden and Bonaparte: General Winter. Schlieffen had not forgotten the fate of Napoleon's *Grande Armeé*, which lost two-thirds of its men during the retreat from Russia in the terrible winter of 1812. Although all generals hoped to emulate Napoleon, Schlieffen had no desire to follow the great Corsican's footsteps in *that* respect.

All things considered, it was clear to Schlieffen that France was the more dangerous foe and, paradoxically, the one who could be defeated more quickly. Since France was a comparatively small country, its armies would be concentrated in a relatively small area. They were sure to be in the north and east at the outset, in

16

position to be enveloped and destroyed in a short, sharp campaign.

Schlieffen therefore proposed that the German Army put its muscle into an overpowering mobile striking force on the right wing, in the north, then launch it along the natural invasion route that had been used by invading armies marching to and from France for centuries: through the Low Countries, specifically Belgium. The weight of this invasion would pivot on Luxembourg and stretch across Belgium to the sea, so that the right wing would overlap the French left before it wheeled inward towards Paris. Schlieffen directed, "Let the last man on the right brush his sleeve in The Channel."

He expected the French to commit the bulk of their forces to attack in Alsace and Lorraine along the Franco-German border, where they would become entangled in the mountains and be unable to extricate themselves in time to meet the blow from the north that would land on their rear and crush them.

As a bonus, the great turning movement of the right wing would also result in the capture of Paris, or at least in isolating the city from the rest of the country. Since practically all the major lines of communication in France, including the railways, ran through the French capital, even if her field armies somehow escaped destruction from the initial blow, France would be virtually paralyzed by this alone. Schlieffen predicted that the campaign to be over in six weeks, with the French Army either compelled to surrender *en masse* or to be so badly mangled as no longer constitute a threat. After that, the bulk of the German divisions could be shipped back east to deal with the Russians who, he calculated, would *still* not be ready.

Count Alfred von Schlieffen was obsessed by his plan. It dominated his thoughts even on his deathbed, in 1913. His last words reputedly were, "Only make the right wing strong.*"* By the time Moltke was appointed

Chief of the General Staff following Schlieffen's retirement in 1906, his predecessor's plan had become the military equivalent of the Gospel: sacred writ. It was no longer a plan; it was The Plan. Moltke approved of The Plan, as both brilliant and, like many other brilliant ideas, simple in conception. He tinkered with the details as the German Army expanded between 1905 and 1914, adding more men to the right wing and also adding strength to the left, but he did not alter the basic pattern.

Moltke assured anyone who asked that The Plan was perfect, but he somehow could not rid himself of certain nagging doubts. It troubled him that the invasion route would go through Belgium, whose neutrality Germany had guaranteed in the Treaty of London in 1839. Moltke was not concerned about the small Belgian Army, which he dismissed as a military nonentity, but he *was* worried about Great Britain.

Britain, like France, Russia, Austria and Prussia (replaced by Germany in 1871), had guaranteed Belgium's perpetual neutrality against any and all invaders. If Germany invaded Belgium, the English were likely to enter the war on the side of the Franco-Russian alliance. Schlieffen had of course been aware of this when he formulated The Plan, but he discounted the ability of the small British Army, expected to be no more than two divisions at the outset, to have any substantial effect on the decisive opening campaign. Schlieffen calculated that by the time the British were able to raise an army big enough to affect the outcome of the war, the French would be beaten and the war in the West would be over.

Moltke himself was not so sure. He believed that a modern, industrialized country like France, when fully mobilized for war, could be defeated only after many months, perhaps even years, of war. He was impressed by the ability of Russia to carry on the war against Japan in 1905, even after its fleets had been shattered and its armies operating at the end of a 3,000-mile supply line.

And Russia was far from being industrialized to the degree that France was.

Moreover, if The Plan miscarried, not only would Germany have to face the army of another Great Power (for given time, the English would surely raise a mass army, if they entered the war), but would also suffer the effects of the inevitable blockade by the Royal Navy, which could prove decisive, if the war did not end as quickly as predicted by Schlieffen.

Schlieffen's operational plan had been inspired by the victory of the Carthaginian general Hannibal at Cannae over the Romans, where 80,000 legionnaires had been slaughtered in a single day, when the Carthaginians enveloped both the Roman flanks. Moltke was not always successful in silencing the little voice that reminded him Carthage had *lost* that war. On his bad days, he could hear the voice of his uncle, the great Field Marshal Moltke, warning, "No plan long survives contact with the enemy."

But it was time to put all the whisperings of doubt behind him, Moltke told himself. The Plan was The Plan, with railway timetables worked out to the minute, intricate arrangements for movement of the great siege guns, and precise scheduling of the each and every element of the invasion, and it was too late to start having second thoughts. The Army was on its way, and The Plan would play itself out, for better or for worse.

Or it would if the armchair generals could keep their hands off the controls and let professional soldiers like himself run the war. But of course, amateur generals *had* to meddle, didn't they? And they most especially had to meddle if the amateur in question was the All-Highest, by the grace of God, Emperor of the Second Reich, Wilhelm II Hohenzollern.

When the Kaiser had, without consulting anyone and completely on his own initiative telegraphed the stop order to General Georg Fuchs, commander of the 16th Division, ordering him not to cross the border until he received authorization from Wilhelm, he threatened to throw the entire war machine into chaos, unless those orders were reversed immediately. Wilhelm had then summoned Moltke to the palace, no doubt to lay out some harebrained scheme of his own design, tossing aside the years of careful planning that had gone into the invasion. .

The Kaiser was a man of many sudden inspirations, most of them ill considered. The General had almost no respect for either the Emperor's judgment or his military abilities. He smiled sourly when he recalled what Count Alfred von Waldersee, a previous Chief of the General Staff, had told the Kaiser after the latter had commanded the "enemy" army in the annual maneuvers back in 1891. Waldersee had crushed the Emperor's forces decisively in the war games, and he evidently had wanted to put an end to the Kaiser's military pretensions for good. During the post-mortem, he had said, "The plan had many traps, and your Majesty fell into every one of them." Of course, Moltke recalled uneasily, Waldersee had been sacked by the Kaiser soon afterward.

He was ushered into Kaiser Wilhelm's presence, followed by his aide Colonel Hentsch. In what had been a library, the Kaiser had set up a War Room, containing an enormous table covered by a map of both the Eastern and Western fronts, complete with little flags on stands indicating the positions of various military units. On the wall overlooking the map table was a full-length portrait of Frederick the Great in full battle array, looking sternly down on his descendant.

The General could see immediately that his sovereign was exultant. The Kaiser was clutching a sheet of blue paper. Since the Foreign Office typically used that type of paper for its official correspondence, Moltke guessed the blue sheet related news of some diplomatic development. (The Kaiser fancied himself to

20

be as talented a diplomat as he was a general, and in this at least, Moltke agreed with him).

"Your Majesty sent for me?" he asked the Kaiser.

Wilhelm turned to him waving the piece of paper, his face flushed with triumph. His eyes flashed and his voice had the peculiarly high pitch it took on when the Emperor was excited. "This is a telegram from our Ambassador in London, Prince Lichnowski. He has a promise from the English Foreign Secretary that they will remain neutral and will keep the French out of the war as well, if we do not attack France!" he exclaimed.

Moltke did not respond. The telegram from London, he knew, was nonsense. The war with France had already been declared: it was too late to undeclare it, no matter what the English Foreign Secretary said. The Kaiser, who had never really accepted the necessity for the invasion of Belgium, was suffering from cold feet and was now trying to use the note from Lichnowski as an excuse to overrule his General Staff and set aside The Plan at the last moment.

Wilhelm paced excitedly back and forth as he spoke, still clutching the telegram. "This is our opportunity to escape the trap! If we invade Belgium, we would surely bring the English in against us. It was the fondest dream of my uncle Edward to destroy Germany, and me in particular. He worked his whole reign to ruin us. Even in death he reaches from the grave to strike down the living me!" he declaimed, gesturing dramatically skyward.

The Kaiser was obsessed with his uncle, the late King Edward VII of Great Britain. King Edward had loved France and the French, and his affection was returned: he was by all odds France's favorite English sovereign. In the course of his many visits to France, both personal and official, Edward had become the face of the new British foreign policy of friendship towards France, which had led to the signing of the Entente

Cordiale in 1904 between the two countries, although he had neither directed nor originated the policy.

Wilhelm had believed for years that Edward was the architect of a scheme to encircle and crush Germany in a ring of enemies. In this he was mistaken, as by the end of the Nineteenth Century the British monarchy had almost no actual power over foreign policy or the governing of the country, but this did not prevent the Kaiser from thinking of and referring to his deceased royal uncle as "the Great Encircler".

The Kaiser continued his tirade. "If we invade Belgium, the onus of the war will fall upon the German people, making *us* appear to be the aggressors in the eyes of the world, when in fact we are only defending our own existence. This was the Great Encircler's plan, the trap he set at our feet, and we must not fall into it!" His voice was rising all through this speech, and by the end he was close to shrieking.

Moltke did not respond and his face remained expressionless. In his experience, the best way to handle the Kaiser when, as now, he was in the throes of inspiration, was to let him run down a little before answering. The Kaiser did not seem to notice the Chief of Staff's lack of enthusiasm. He waved Moltke over to the big map table, and jabbed his finger at the mountainous French border.

"We are expecting the French to attack here, are you not?" the Kaiser asked, pointing his finger and sweeping his arm from Thionville in Lorraine, just south of Luxembourg, down to Mulhouse, a little north of the Swiss border. The majority of the little flag stands bearing the tri-color of France were clustered along that serpentine line, based on Intelligence reports that the bulk of the French Army was stationed along the frontier between Germany and France.

"Yes, Your Majesty," Moltke replied patiently. "So far as we know, the French have most of their strength concentrated between Sedan and the Swiss border. It is

22

possible that their Fourth Army will attempt to attack in the Ardennes as well, in reaction to our entry into Belgium." The General's finger brushed the southern corner of Belgium on the map.

"Ha! Let *them* attack the neutral first," the Kaiser exulted. "Then see if the English will come to pull their chestnuts from the fire." He paused. "We have adequate troops in that region to handle a French invasion, I suppose," he said thoughtfully, looking at the symbols for the units of the German Sixth and Seventh Armies in Alsace and Lorraine.

Moltke sighed. "We have ..." he calculated silently, "720,000 men available on that sector of the front, most of them in fortifications. If necessary, we could even shift a corps from the Crown Prince's army, if there seemed to be any danger of a breakthrough. Intelligence estimates that the maximum number of men the French have available for offensive operations in that region is between 650,000 and 750,000. They will not break through our positions in Alsace, or Lorraine, for that matter. But..."

"Don't you see what this means, General?" the Kaiser continued. The pitch of his voice began to rise again, and his eyes flashed as he grew more excited. He waved the note from the Foreign Office again. "Don't you see the opportunity we have? This..." the blue paper crackled as the Kaiser shook it vigorously, "...destroys any excuse the warmongers in England have to attack us. We will stand fast in the West, and send the right wing to the East to smash the Russians! If the French want to attack us, let them bloody their noses in the mountains. Let *them* invade Belgium, and the world will see who the true warmongers are. Who knows, if the French are foolish enough to violate Belgium, perhaps the English will declare war on them! And if they do not, why then, we will have only the Russian enemy to defeat, as the French are impotent to injure us

23

and, best of all, there will be no excuse for my English cousins to engage in the war!"

Moltke decided that the time had come to deflate his sovereign. "Your Majesty, it cannot be done," he told the Kaiser. "The deployment of millions of men cannot be improvised. If Your Majesty insists on massive changes to the plan at this late date, you will not have an army ready for battle, but a disorganized mob of armed men with no arrangements for supply. Those arrangements took a whole year of intricate planning to complete, and once settled they cannot be altered."

The Kaiser, derailed by this display of military expertise, had no reply. The enthusiasm seemed to rush out of him like the air from a punctured balloon, and he slowly sank into a convenient chair, gazing across the room at nothing.

The General gestured to Colonel Hentsch, who opened the briefcase and handed Moltke the written order the latter had prepared for the 16th Division to resume its advance into Luxembourg. He held it out to Wilhelm and said, "Your Majesty *must* sign this order."

As soon as the words left his mouth, Moltke wanted to take them back. The Kaiser, who had appeared to have run down like a clock whose mainspring had unwound, now suddenly sprang back to life. He rose quickly to his feet, and fixed a glare on his presumptuous subordinate. His face was dark red, his lips drawn back in a scowl. He was as furious as Moltke had ever seen him.

"*Your... Majesty... must?*" he repeated slowly, emphasizing each word, his eyes flashing.

The Chief of the General Staff stuttered, "Your Majesty, I simply meant..."

The Kaiser began in ominously low tones. "*You* dare to tell *me* what I '*must*' do with *my* army, here in the Palace of the Hohenzollerns?" His voice rose until the last few words were almost bellowed. He paused, and then continued in a tone that suggested rage only

24

barely contained. "I will tell *you* about 'must', General. *You* must follow the commands of your sovereign. *You* must produce for my signature a plan that will send my armies to East Prussia against the Russians instead of idiotically violating Belgium, a plan that will provide for all their supplies, ammunition and anything else they will need to fight. Today is Saturday. *You* must have this plan ready for my signature by midnight Sunday or I will have a new Chief of Staff Monday morning."

"But Your Majesty…" Moltke began again.

The Kaiser cut him short with a sharp chopping motion of his hand. "Can you guarantee me victory over France in two months if we follow your fabulous plan?" He paused to study Moltke's face. "Can you *guarantee* it, General?" he asked again, sharply.

Moltke hesitated. He uneasily recalled a long discussion he had had with the Kaiser two years earlier concerning the next war. Moltke had discoursed at length about his belief that any war between modern Great Powers would be long and difficult, and would exhaust the victors nearly as much as it would the losers. This belief directly contravened the key premise of The Plan, that modern, industrialized France could be defeated quickly in a short, sharp war. There was nothing wrong with Wilhelm's memory. Wilhelm knew well enough that his Chief of the General Staff was himself far from convinced that France would be knocked out in the six weeks promised by The Plan.

"Your Majesty knows that there are no guarantees in wartime…" Moltke said, trailing off.

The Kaiser waited long enough to see if the General had anything more to add before he continued with growing confidence in his decision. "Now, we have a General Staff that in peacetime constantly makes and revises plans for every possible contingency. There is a plan for a war with Russia only, with France only, with France and England, with the United States, with Austria, with invaders from the Moon, most probably.

25

You have a Director of the Military Railways on your staff, what's his name, von Stamm…?"

"Staab," Moltke corrected.

"Yes, that's the one, von Staab. He does nothing but prepare alternative train schedules for all these contingencies. That is the principal function of the Director of the Military Railways, is it not? I must therefore believe that somewhere in his files and in the files of the General Staff are alternative arrangements for the movements I am now ordering you to make."

The Sovereign was right about the contingency plans, of course. General Herman von Staab, Chief of the Military Railways, had prepared alternate plans for every conceivable contingency, as had his fellow department heads on the General Staff. Just last week, Moltke had reviewed a plan to seize the mountain passes in Northern Switzerland, in the event the need to invade France south of Mulhouse arose. That was about as likely to happen as… as an invasion from the Moon, but there was a plan for it. There was no doubt that von Staab had a plan in his files with rail schedules and train assignments for the transfer all the men, guns and supplies that had been ticketed for France via Belgium to Prussia that would send them all East instead, exactly as the Kaiser wanted

The mercurial Wilhelm was buoyant and overflowing with self-assurance at having won this debate over military strategy with his general. His tone now shifted from the argumentative to the inspirational. He struck a histrionic pose and began to speak as if addressing a large audience.

"This is the moment of supreme crisis for the German nation, General, the supreme moment of your career! Think what your uncle the great Field Marshal would have done, and act as he would have. Our gallant men at arms, all our people, our very national existence, all depend on *you*. Go, and do your duty to Kaiser and country!" The Kaiser pointed dramatically. "You are dismissed."

"It shall be as you command, Your Majesty," Moltke gritted out through clenched teeth. He snapped to attention, saluted, spun on his heel and marched from the room, with Hentsch following.

They walked unspeaking for a while, the only sound the clack of their boots on the marble floor. Then Hentsch said, "For a minute, I was sure he was going to buy that business about it being too late to make changes. Wilhelm may not be Frederick the Great, but he does understand the function of the General Staff."

Moltke, whose face had been gradually turning the color of a ripe tomato, suddenly exploded. "Why is it Hentsch, that a *civilian*, an *amateur*, a man without the time, inclination or training for strategic thought, believes that *he* is qualified to set aside a war plan prepared by *professionals*? If the royal yacht ran into a storm, would he try to seize the wheel away from the ship's captain?"

"War is far too important to be left to politicians," Hentsch agreed. He continued, in a philosophical vein, "Still, what is done is done, and we must go on from here."

As he strode through the halls of the *Stadschloss*, Moltke's temper began to cool, and he pondered the simple truth in Hentsch's words. The decision had been made, whether for good or ill only time would tell, and there was no turning back. He reflected that the Director of the Military Railways was going to arrange the delivery of nearly three-quarters of a million fighting men to the border of Russian Poland in about two weeks, and it would be well to have something for those men to do while they were there, besides picking wild strawberries. He frowned more deeply than ever, and quickened his pace.

Chapter Two: London, August 4, 1914

It was late afternoon, and the bright sunshine bathing King Charles Street was slanting down at a shallow angle through the window of his private office at Whitehall by the time Sir Edward Grey finally completed his last correspondence of the day. It was a note to his Ambassador in Brussels, requesting whatever new information was available concerning German military movements on the border of Belgium.

Grey shook a little sand onto the paper to absorb any excess ink, then carefully folded it and slid it into a Foreign Office envelope. He thoughtfully ran his thumb over the gold embossed lion and, wishing that he could do more to aid his beleaguered French allies meet the looming European crisis than write notes to his Ambassadors, placed the envelope in the battered red leather dispatch box that would carry it to Belgium.

Grey had been appointed to his present post in 1905, and had remained the Foreign Secretary ever since, serving in the Liberal government of Sir Henry Campbell-Bannerman and then staying on under his successor, Herbert Asquith. He had continued the European policies that he had inherited from predecessors. In particular, he had broadened the agreements with France and Russia that had been negotiated in 1904 and 1907 by Lord Lansdowne and Sir Arthur Nicolson, which together constituted the Triple Entente.

This arrangement was not quite a formal alliance between the three countries. France and Russia had a true and binding alliance with each other, which included a military convention promising that each would go to war if the other was attacked by a third power. Great Britain had no such agreement with either France or Russia, or anybody else, for that matter.

Grey would have had it otherwise. He was a man of peace, who had no desire to involve his country in a war between Great Powers, which he believed would be a disaster for European civilization. But, he was convinced that if Great Britain was known to be firmly committed to the Franco-Russian Entente, this might be enough to cause Germany to back down, thus averting a crisis without resorting to war. On the other hand, if there was going to be a war, it was clearly not in Britain's national interest to allow the German-dominated Triple Alliance to prevail. The consequences of *that* would be...

Grey's musings were interrupted by a knock on his office door. His private secretary said, "Please excuse the interruption, Sir Edward. The French Ambassador, his Excellency, Monsieur Cambon, has arrived for his appointment. Shall I show him in?"

This was a meeting that Grey had been dreading all day. A feeling of guilt settled heavily over him, even though he knew he had done everything in his power to try to make the French alliance a reality, and that his failure to do so was not through any lack of effort on his part.

Grey was one of the members of the faction in the Cabinet who had been promoting closer ties with France for years. He and his group had all but promised the French that they could count on the Royal Navy to cover the French Channel ports in the event of war with Germany. They had even arranged joint General Staff talks and the preparation of a non-binding military convention between the two countries.

Grey, along with everyone else, had assumed that when the war began, the Germans would provide a *casus belli* by invading Belgium, thus bringing in Great Britain under obligations the latter had taken on as a guarantor of Belgian neutrality in the Treaty of London of 1839. It was common knowledge in European military and diplomatic circles that the Germans were planning to

29

launch their invasion of France through Belgium. Certainly, the Kaiser and his minions had made enough suggestive and threatening remarks to Belgian officials (up to and including King Albert himself) over the last few years to lead Grey to expect that the Germans to violate Belgian territory at the onset of hostilities. When that happened, Grey was prepared to go to the House of Commons and ask for a declaration of war based on Britain's national interests, her treaty commitment to Belgium, and her national honor.

Two days earlier, on August 1, Grey had sent a Note to the German ambassador to Great Britain, Prince Karl Max Lichnowski. The statement was vague and promised little. This was for two reasons. The first was that Grey was painfully aware he had no authority from his Government to commit Great Britain to any course of action in the Continental crisis, even if Belgium was invaded.

The second reason was that it was Grey's preferred diplomatic style to be vague. He believed that the less precise one's language, the more room one had to maneuver as needed. It was practically his motto.

Grey had told Prince Lichnowski that he could guarantee England's neutrality if Germany would remain neutral as to both France and Russia, in other words, not go to war at all. This was not much of a commitment; in fact, it was really no commitment at all. Grey had not thought that this offer would make the slightest impression on the Germans.

Instead, this innocuous pledge appeared to have induced the Germans to pull back their troop concentrations from the Belgian frontier and send their armies...elsewhere. The German Ambassador was known to be a strong advocate of peace, one of the few who had any influence on his country's foreign policy. He wondered what Prince Lichnowski had told his Foreign Ministry.

The German withdrawal from the Belgian border was, in Grey's view, unfortunate. Without a German invasion of Belgium, there was no possibility that Great Britain would come into the war on the side of France. The House of Commons would never agree to go to war to help either the Russians or the French without some further provocation. Whatever the reason behind it, the withdrawal had been a clever stroke by the Germans. It had pulled the rug out from under Grey and his Francophile allies in the Cabinet.

Now, he was going to have to tell Ambassador Cambon that His Majesty's Government was "...unable to commit to any definite action under the present circumstances..." Grey muttered to himself. "In other words, we plan to do a fair imitation of rats leaving a sinking ship," he finished bitterly.

"The French Ambassador is here, sir," Grey's private secretary said.

"Show Monsieur Cambon in please, Harrison," Grey said.

Grey's secretary disappeared, and then returned a few moments later to announce, "His Excellency, Ambassador Paul Cambon."

"Thank you, Harrison," Grey said, dismissing his subordinate. The private secretary bowed to Grey, then to Cambon, and left silently.

Paul Cambon was a dapper figure, with short, wiry gray hair and a neatly trimmed beard and mustache. Grey considered the Frenchman to be a personal friend more than a diplomatic colleague. They had met at a party in 1895 just after Cambon had first taken up his current post, and the two men developed an immediate liking and respect for each other. Since 1905, when Grey had come to the Foreign office, they had worked closely together, trying to arrange a military alliance between their nations, trying in vain, as events proved.

Now the Frenchman stood rigid, his face expressionless, his eyes fixed on Grey's. Grey himself felt stiff and uncomfortable in his friend's presence.

"It is a pleasure to see you again, Paul," Grey said. He gestured to a Louis XIV armchair embroidered with hunting scenes. The chair had been a birthday present from Cambon on the occasion of Grey's 40th birthday. "Please, make yourself comfortable."

"No thank you, Mr. Foreign Secretary," responded the Frenchman icily. "My errand will not take long."

Grey cringed inwardly when the other man addressed him formally, rather than by his first name, as he had done for so many years. This interview which he had been dreading all day was beginning quite as badly as he had anticipated. Long years of diplomatic practice allowed Grey to maintain an impassive mask that hid the pain he felt, although he could not control the way his complexion paled.

There was a long, uncomfortable silence. When Cambon finally spoke again, his voice was strained. "I am here, as you must know, Mr. Foreign Secretary, to ascertain the position of His Majesty's Government with regard to commitments previously made by your Government to France. Promises, mutual obligations between our Governments were made ten years ago, and have since been renewed and extended. The time has come to redeem those commitments, now that Germany has declared an unprovoked war on my country." He paused. Grey waited, saying nothing.

"Does His Majesty's Government intend to place the Royal Navy on station in the English Channel to cover French ports as was previously arranged?" Cambon demanded. "What is the prospect of fulfilling the terms of the military convention between our countries? His Majesty's Government was committed to landing the British Expeditionary Force in Channel ports in cooperation with the left wing of the French Army. This was part of our mutual war plans. When will these troops be landing? The war has begun; our plans must take into account the intentions of our allies."

There was another endless period of silence, which lasted perhaps three seconds. Grey knew that he had no satisfactory answer, that he had nothing to offer the anguished Frenchman.

"Surely, Paul, you and the French Government understood that all of those arrangements were on an informal basis," he replied steadily. "His Majesty's Government has never undertaken a formal commitment to go to war alongside France. In point of fact, such a commitment would not have been approved by the Cabinet or Parliament, as you well know. All of these arrangements were contingent upon the occurrence of certain events over which we have no control. The informal arrangements were the best that we could manage. Indeed, we had to take care to see that even the informal arrangements did not become general knowledge, to prevent a public outcry against Continental commitments. A military alliance with France, with any Continental Power, has never been a popular idea in this country."

"So, His Majesty's Government intends to stand aside and do nothing at this critical moment in history? Will you simply look on with arms folded while the German Empire comes to dominate Europe?" demanded the Ambassador, his voice quavering with emotion. "Because if you wait until *after* we and the Russians are crushed, it will then be far too late to do anything. The shadow of Prussianism will fall over the whole of the Continent. What will His Majesty's Government do then, with France and Russia defeated and prostrate, and a hostile German Empire supreme? What will you do then, Monsieur Foreign Secretary?"

Grey's mouth tightened, but his voice was calm as always. It was a little unfair of Cambon to blame Grey for the apparent abandonment of the French by His Majesty's Government. It was only because he and a handful of colleagues in the Cabinet had insisted that anything at all had been done. As he had reminded Cambon, the informal understanding with France had been the absolute most they could achieve under the circumstances. The simple truth was that, if not for the informal arrangements, they would have had nothing at all. As events turned out, that was exactly what they *did* have: nothing.

Still, he did not blame Cambon. If their positions were reversed, Grey suspected that he would feel exactly the same way as the Frenchman did.

Normally Grey held as an article of faith that he was morally bound to support the positions of his own government. If he could not do so, then his personal sense of honor required him to resign rather than remain in office in a false position. But on this occasion, Grey's feelings of guilt were so strong that he felt compelled to violate this rule, by admitting to Cambon that his own views were at variance with those of the government he served.

"You know I wish it were otherwise, and that I believe we should come to France's aid in her hour of peril, but my personal feelings on the matter are of no consequence," he said. "It is the official position of His Majesty's Government that a quarrel between Russia, Austria, Germany and France is not a matter of vital interest to Great Britain sufficient to constitute a *casus belli*. It is absolutely clear that neither in Parliament nor among the public is there any support for taking the country into the war under the present circumstances."

He sighed. "I should tell you that two days ago a group of Liberal MPs voted 19 to 4 to remain neutral, *even if Germany were to violate Belgium*. The Cabinet has already voted 12 to 6 against going to war in support of France, and further decided to not even allow the fleet to take up war stations in the North Sea for fear of provoking an incident with the German Navy. Mr. Asquith will never take a divided country into war;

indeed, he could not even if he wished to, as support for such a course does not exist in Parliament. We must await some new development before the Prime Minister can even consider putting the question to the House or the Cabinet. There is really nothing we can do but wait for new developments, and hope."

Ambassador Cambon burst out, "Kaiser Wilhelm is not going to oblige us by invading Belgium. There is not going to *be* any 'new development'. So what will happen now? Based on your country's assurances, all our military plans were arranged in common, on the assumption that Great Britain would be fighting at our side. Those plans are now in ruins. Our General Staffs have consulted and you have seen our schemes and preparations. Our fleet has committed to the Mediterranean and we have left our Atlantic coast wide open to the Germans, all because of British guarantees. If you abandon us now, France will never forgive you. What will be the value of English promises after this betrayal, and what allies will rely on them in the future?"

Grey had no answers for the anguished Cambon. The fact of the matter was that he agreed with everything the Frenchman said. He subscribed the adage attributed to his predecessor, Lord Palmerston, that Britain had neither permanent friends nor permanent enemies, only permanent interests. The most important permanent interest, the guiding star of British foreign policy in Europe for generations, had been to oppose the domination of the Continent by any single power, and to ally with the lesser powers to prevent such domination. The British Empire had joined coalitions against the Hapsburgs in the 17th century, against Louis XIV, the Sun King, in the 18[th,] and had headed the alliance that finally defeated Napoleon in the last century, guided by that same principle. Would she now allow the German Empire to succeed where the others had failed? As he accompanied the Frenchman from his office, he could only say, "Let us hope that tomorrow brings better tidings." Cambon did not reply.

Grey sat for a long time in his office after the French Ambassador had left, reading new intelligence estimates from the War Ministry about Belgium. Nothing he read gave him any comfort at all. Every source available to the British government; diplomats, military observers and newspaper reporters, all told the same story: massive formations of German troops were pulling out from the Belgian border and boarding trains rolling off to... where? To the East, to Prussia, to fight the Russians was what nearly everyone thought.

Grey pondered whether he should offer his resignation to the Prime Minister. He was strongly tempted to take some action to demonstrate his feelings, and he thought it would be a great relief to be rid of the responsibilities of the Ministry. In the end, he decided that resignation would amount to no more than a gesture, and would do nothing to change his country's course. He was too responsible to commit such a rash act just to allay his personal sense of guilt.

Long after evening had fallen and the streetlamps on Downing Street flickered to life, Grey brooded over his meeting with the French Ambassador. Cambon was right, he decided. Without British help, the Franco-Russian coalition would eventually be overwhelmed, and an aggressive, militaristic Germany, with a growing population, expanding industry and ambition to match, would come to dominate Europe. "*Then* what will we do?" Grey murmured aloud, echoing the words of the departed French Ambassador. "Then what?"

Chapter Three: Berlin, August 6, 1914

Under ordinary circumstances, Ray Swing would have gladly spent a few hours of a steamy August Berlin afternoon here in the Pratergarten in the fashionable Prenzlauer Berg district. The beer garden had been brewing and serving its own beer since it opened in 1837, and nowhere in the city could a tastier glass of beer be had. Moreover, the linden trees provided a cool, shady place to rest, the chairs were comfortable, the *wursts* among the best in town, and even the inevitable brass band that Germans seemed to feel was an essential part of the beer-drinking experience, was neither as loud nor as annoying as its counterparts at rival beer gardens.

But Swing would be hard-pressed to come up with a word that was less appropriate than "ordinary" to describe *this* August, in the summer of 1914. Ray Swing was a journalist, and pure luck had landed him in Berlin right in the middle of the biggest story since Napoleon's defeat at Waterloo. The capital of the German Empire was this summer the epicenter of the greatest European war in more than a century and, as the newly appointed (three months) chief of German bureau of the *Chicago Daily News*, it was his job to report on the conflagration for readers back in America.

During the preceding week, he had closely followed the progress of the German mobilization in his dispatches home. He had described the rivers of the Kaiser's *feldgrau*-clad soldiers flowing through the streets of Berlin as the cheers of the happy citizenry rang in their ears, the pretty women showering the marching men with flowers or running up to kiss a lucky trooper, the endless troop trains overflowing with the young Teutonic warriors waving out the windows, laughing and singing as if the war would be some wonderful vacation or a glorious game.

But Swing's role was no longer just that of a reporter. As bureau chief, he was also obliged to oversee the work of his all-too-few reporters whom he had dispatched to cover as many of the scattered potential battlefields as possible, and to coordinate their reports so that they were reasonably consistent (or at least, not completely inconsistent), when they were put together for publication.

In short, there was enough work to keep three Ray Swings busy around the clock. Yet, in the middle of the unfolding European apocalypse, he had agreed to take two hours that he did not have to spare for a meeting in this beer garden. There was only one reason he had done so: because of his friendship and respect for the man who had asked him to meet today, Joseph Stilwell.

Even as Swing brooded, he saw the man himself moving smoothly through the lindens and around the tables filled with sweating burghers gulping down massive one liter steins of the house summer beer, heading for Swing's table. The thirty-one year old First Lieutenant (not for the first time, Swing reflected on the slow pace of promotions in the peacetime American Army), was a thin, wiry man, with an alert expression on his intelligent face, a sharp beak of a nose and a piercing, compelling gaze. His upright military posture made him appear to be taller than his actual five feet, eight inches. He was not in uniform today, but was dressed in a white linen suit topped by a Panama hat.

Stilwell sat at the table and removed his hat, using it to fan his perspiring face. He ordered a beer by catching the eye of one of the powerfully built *bierkellnerins* who was rushing by with two foaming glass steins in each hand, and holding up one finger. The hefty *fraulein* smiled, nodded and said, "*Einen moment bitte, mein Herr,*" then hurried on.

"Sorry to keep you waiting, Ray," he apologized, "but the poor Ambastador is about to go completely off his rails from the overwork. It seems that the State

38

Department keeps insisting that he supply them with daily updated reports on the political and military situation over here, and his position is that if he wanted to work for a living, he would never have gone into politics."

Stilwell had a low opinion of the abilities of his boss (an opinion fully shared by Swing), Ambassador Extraordinary and Plenipotentiary to the Empire of Germany by appointment of the President of the United States of America on the advice and consent of the Senate, the Honorable James W. Gerard. He considered Gerard to be nothing more than a life-long political hack who had received the appointment as a reward for his years of service in the corrupt Tammany Hall Democratic machine. It would have gone without saying that Stilwell thought Gerard was completely unqualified for the position, except for the military attaché's inability to keep his opinion of the Ambassador to himself.

"I haven't been here long enough to finish even one lager," Swing replied, holding aloft a half-full stein. "I'm not surprised about the... *Ambassador*... you really should stop using that nickname, you know. The wrong person is going to hear you one of these days... but I am curious about what would bring the military attaché of the American Embassy out to a beer garden at such a critical time, and in mufti at that."

Before replying, Stilwell swiveled his head right and left to look around the garden through the haze of cigar smoke at the stolid German citizenry enjoying tankards of beer, plates of *spätzle* and sausage. Seeing nothing to arouse his suspicions, he said quietly, "I have new orders from Washington, straight from the War Department. The... *Ambassador*..." he pronounced the word with extravagant care, making a sour face as he did so, "...knows nothing about them." He looked at Swing meaningfully.

At this moment, the waitress returned to thump a great mug of foaming pale beer in front of Stilwell. He laid a silver one-mark coin in her hand, making a gesture to indicate that she was to keep the excess fifty *pfennigs* as a gratuity. The waitress clasped her hands together and gasped in astonishment at such largess.

"*Oh danke, mein Herr! Dankeshon!*" she exclaimed.

"*Es ist nichts,*" the American said modestly, motioning for her to resume her duties.

The two men speculatively regarded the beer-maiden's solidly built posterior as she walked away. Swing said, "Joe, I think if you asked her out for a date tonight, you might get lucky."

"She's not my type," Stilwell replied, shaking his head. "She'd probably break my arm if she got excited in a clinch." He returned his gaze to his companion. "Now, where was I? Oh yeah, the new orders from DepWar."

"I'm going to guess they want you gather some intelligence on the German army," Swing said.

"They want me to make personal observations of the Kraut war machine in action," Stilwell replied. "They want my evaluations of everything from combat morale to infantry-artillery coordination to how they load heavy equipment on their troop trains."

"I've seen that last one," Swing volunteered. "They do it very cleverly. They open up the ends of all the cars, lay down planks between them and then roll the guns or whatever all the way through to the first car. Then to unload…"

"I know. I've seen it myself," Stilwell said. "I heard that the Kaiser himself gave the Army the idea, after he saw the Ringling Brothers Circus load up that way."

"Anyway, I don't see why your orders are so hush-hush," Swing said. "That would be a normal assignment for an attaché of a neutral power in wartime, wouldn't it?"

"Right, but there's a little bit more," Stilwell said. He leaned forward. "The War Department has information that the Krauts are working on new weapons."

"Like what, exactly?" Swing asked. "I don't suppose you're talking about using their zeppelins to drop explosives from the air? From what I hear, they wouldn't be very practical in combat. Too inaccurate, and the bomb loads they could carry would be too small to accomplish much anyway. It's no secret the Germans have been thinking about it."

"How about a gadget that throws burning fuel fifty yards through the air, sticks to skin and clothing like glue, and can't be put out with water?" Stilwell asked.

Swing's eyes opened wide as he responded. "Burned to death with liquid fire? Christ, that's horrible! Don't they have enough nasty ways to kill each other yet?"

"Maybe not," the attaché said grimly. "There are rumors that their chemists are also developing some kind of asphyxiating gas, which will burn the lungs out of anybody who breathes it."

The journalist considered the effects of deadly clouds of gas descending on unsuspecting soldiers, briefly picturing men writhing in the mud, coughing and suffocating in their own blood. He swallowed.

"Ok," he said at last. "I agree it's important, but I'm just a reporter, Joe. What do you want me to do for you, write a feature article for the Sunday edition about the Kaiser's secret weapons?" he inquired ironically.

"My orders are to set up an intelligence network here," Stilwell explained. "I know you have contacts in Germany who would never deal directly with an American officer. We need to learn more about these weapons, their state of operational readiness for use in the field, and anything else you can get." Seeing his friend's expression, Stilwell paused.

"Listen, Ray, I know this isn't your job," he continued. "I won't blame you if you say 'no'. Just let me say my piece, and I'll never bring it up again."

Swing nodded. "Go ahead."

"The German Empire is a real world power, with the best army in the world and maybe the second-best navy. They have the best chemists, the best metallurgists, the best technology in the world. The people are hard workers, smart, productive and well educated. Their leaders are aggressive, and they are not afraid to use their military power to get what they want, not afraid to start a war for it." Stilwell paused again, looking at Swing for his reaction.

"I agree with everything you said, but..." Swing began.

"If Germany wins this war, don't you think there's a pretty good chance that we, the United States, will have to take them on somewhere down the road?" Stilwell asked. "Don't forget that we almost had a war with them back in '98 over the Philippines."

Stilwell was referring to a run-in between Commodore George Dewey and a squadron of German cruisers under Rear Admiral Otto von Diederichs off the Philippines just after Dewey had annihilated the Spanish Asiatic Fleet in the Battle of Manila Bay. The German squadron began maneuvering as if intending to claim the islands, taking advantage of destruction of the Spanish fleet. In that instance, with the powerful British Asiatic Fleet quietly supporting the Americans, the outgunned Diederichs had prudently chosen to withdraw.

Stilwell continued grimly, "Now add these Greek fire gadgets and poisonous gas, and a few other things we don't know about yet. Ray, our country isn't ready for a war with Germany. I don't know when we will be. We need every bit of information we can get, so that when we do go at it with them (and it's *when* we do, not *if*, for my money), we won't be caught with our pants down. It isn't hard to see how important that is, is it?"

42

Stilwell hoisted his beer and finished what remained in the stein in one long swallow. Swing absently regarded his companion's bobbing Adam's apple as the last drops of the Pratergarten wheat beer vanished down the military attaché's gullet.

"Well, I've done my patriotic duty, trying to enlist you," he said at last, nudging a few spots of foam from his upper lip with a knuckle, "and I won't say I blame you the least bit for turning me down. Once this war really gets going, you're going to be busier than a one-armed paperhanger with the hives. Did your credentials to travel with the German Army ever come through?" He changed the subject, as if the question of the spy network was now settled and forgotten.

Swing did not respond immediately. He removed his rimless glasses from his nose, wiped the condensed droplets of water from the lenses and replaced them, carefully hooking the earpieces in place. Then he looked down at the heavy beer mug in his hand for a few seconds, and said slowly, "I think I may have changed my mind about helping you out. The more I consider it, the less I like the idea of a triumphant German Empire," Swing said. "I have the impression that the more they get, the more they will demand: territory here in Europe, colonies overseas, trade privileges in the Far East, and who knows what next? I agree with you: there is going be a showdown with the German Empire someday, maybe not too far in the future, and I don't want us to be on the losing side. I've traveled in Alsace and seen the way they treat non-Germans unlucky enough to fall under the rule of the Empire, and I don't want that for the U.S.A."

Stilwell nodded. "Okay, good. I'll get some leads for you in the War Ministry and, by the way, there's some money available for you and whoever you recruit."

He relaxed, easing back in his seat. "So, what's your take on the latest Kraut troop movements? Last week, every troop train in the country was headed west, and now they're all coming back again. You don't suppose Kaiser Willy realized that the war was a mistake and has called the whole thing off, do you?" he asked sardonically.

Swing smiled. "That doesn't seem very likely," he said. "For some reason... who knows why?... it looks like Moltke has scotched the invasion of Belgium and is shipping most of his right wing east to fight the Russians."

The German plan of beginning the campaign in the West by invading her tiny neighbor in violation of the Treaty of London, had been an open secret for years. The Germans had been intimidating the Belgians for some time, even to the extent of the German ambassador personally warning (threatening, really) King Albert that he would be wise to order his army not to resist in the event of a German invasion.

"Could it be that somebody upstairs in the German government had a rush of brains to the head, and saw that violating Belgium was about the only sure way of bringing the British into the war against them?" Swing speculated.

"If so, it would be just about the first sign of intelligence in the Chancellery since the Kaiser 'dropped the pilot'..." Stilwell said. The Kaiser had dismissed the Iron Chancellor, Otto von Bismarck, the architect of the German Empire under Wilhelm I, the current Kaiser's grandfather in 1890. "...and that was almost twenty-five years ago."

Swing did not venture to disagree with this assessment. German foreign policy had been notoriously erratic under the guidance of Bismarck's successors. It was widely believed that the Kaiser himself was responsible for most, if not all, of the thumb-fingered diplomatic moves over the last quarter-century that had given the German Empire an international reputation as a loose cannon and the Kaiser one as a dangerous warmonger.

44

Swing's impression was that Wilhelm II was not a stupid man, nor an evil one, but simply impulsive.

"It may just be another one of Wilhelm's brainstorms," Swing hazarded. "A pretty good one for Germany, too, if you ask me."

Stilwell said nothing, merely grunting to indicate his agreement as he raised his hand to signal the hefty *bierkellnerin,* this time raising two fingers.

"I have time for one more before I have to go back to work for the great statesman and diplomat from New York, *Ambassador...*" again he pronounced the word with sarcastic precision, "...James W. Gerard. Another beer *might* make him almost bearable," he concluded.

Chapter Four: Near Nancy, August 21, 1914

"The whole Fifteenth Corps is running away, General." Major Jean Hughes of the Second Army staff had been sent out by HQ to get a firsthand report on the fighting in the mountains east of Morhange, where the French offensive had been held up by German resistance. He was now reporting over the telephone to the Army Commander, General deCastlenau, describing sights that he had never thought he would see. "If I have ever seen beaten men in my life, then I am looking at them now."

The offensive in Lorraine, the northern half of Plan XVII, had started promisingly four days earlier. The Second Army's thrust through the Vosges Mountains toward the initial objective, the rail junction at the town of Morhange, had advanced ahead of schedule, brushing aside light German opposition. Some of the more exuberant French commanders claimed that the *boches* were already beaten and would offer no resistance this side of the Rhine, and perhaps not even on the far side.

Hughes, examining the reports at Second Army HQ, was dubious about these claims. The normal signs of a defeated enemy, masses of prisoners and captured guns, were nowhere to be found. Hughes and his Intelligence Section colleagues believed that the Germans were simply drawing the invaders into the mountains to fight it out on ground of their own choosing. Hughes predicted that the Germans would stand and fight in the wooded slopes of the mountains east of Morhange.

The leading elements of the Second Army entered Morhange on the 18th, and rapidly occupied the undefended town. The soldiers rejoiced at the liberation of this corner of the Lost Province: they were the first French soldiers to set foot in the city since Germany had wrenched Lorraine and its sister province Alsace from France more than forty years earlier as part of the shameful peace treaty that ended the Franco-Prussian War. That war was referred to in France, when it was spoken of at all, as *le debacle*.

The headlines in every newspaper from Calais to Marseille screamed "*Revanche*!" in thick, black letters. The accompanying articles assumed that the despised Huns were fleeing, and the liberation of Alsace and Lorraine was all but accomplished.

On the morning of third day, the advance of the Second Army came to an abrupt halt in the wooded hills two kilometers east of Morhange. The commander of the 15th Corps, General Gerard, who on the previous day been certain the Germans were routed, now reported that enemy artillery fire had inflicted such heavy casualties on his corps that it would be incapable of offensive action for at least 48 hours. There were similar reports from other corps commanders, indicating stiff German resistance all along the Second Army front. DeCastlenau peremptorily ordered them to continue to attack until the German positions were penetrated.

By the afternoon, the Second Army's assaults had been hurled back along the line. General deCastlenau decided he needed an eyewitness account from an officer he could trust. He recalled that Hughes had predicted that the *boches* would dig in east of Morhange, and ordered the Intelligence man up to the front to make a first-hand observation.

The Major rode a staff car up to 15th Corps headquarters just outside Morhange to talk to General Gerard. The 15th Corps commanding officer complained that his assault columns were being blasted apart by German artillery almost as soon as they formed to launch an attack.

"Their guns outrange ours, and they hold all the high ground. So, when I try to soften the *boches* up with a preliminary bombardment, the counter-battery fire just

47

blows my 75s all to Hell, Major," explained the General. "When we attack without any artillery preparation…" he gestured east. "I suggest you go up there to see for yourself. I am not saying that what General deCastlenau is asking is impossible, but… Go up and see. The 29th Division is putting in another attack."

Hughes left the agitated Gerard, and went up to an observation post of the 29th Division to watch the French attack through field glasses.

As Gerard had said, the *poilus* were already under heavy shelling before they even reached the start line. Explosions ripped gaps in the French formations, leaving bodies scattered on the hillside. The attackers continued to dress their lines and fill in the gaps until they reached the jumping-off point, at the base of a steep, thickly wooded hill.

Now the junior officers that led the assault jumped up, fiercely blowing their whistles and waving their men forward to the attack. Many of these brave, young officers were hit by German fire right away, as they were conspicuously out in front of the men they led. Hughes noted that in the gloom of the forest, the French soldiers' bright red trousers stood out remarkably well, and undoubtedly made tempting targets for the German riflemen and machine-gunners. The gray-clad Germans, on the other hand, were much harder to see.

He watched as the men who charged up the steep slope with fixed bayonets were cut to pieces long before they could get into bayonet range. The Germans had set up machine-gun nests with interlocking fields of fire that covered every approach to the summit. Every fallen log, every pile of rocks seemed to have been converted into a strongpoint from which the deadly Maxim guns spit out streams of death. Here and there, whether by phenomenal courage, unusual skill or blind luck, a group of French soldiers were able to close with a German pillbox or machine-gun nest and take it out with hand grenades and rifle fire at point blank range, but for the

48

most part, the attackers were simply scythed down before they could get near the enemy. In twenty minutes, the slope was littered with dead bodies and the attack had collapsed. The survivors retreated sullenly back down to the shallow trenches at the base of the hill where they had started, carrying or dragging their dead and wounded comrades with them.

The French tactical scheme was a complete disaster, Hughes decided. He recalled the *Ecole Superior de la Guerre* lectures he had attended before the war, given by Colonel (now Brigadier General) Grandmaison on the power of the offensive, the so-called *offensive à outrance*. "The French soldier *must* triumph in battle because his superior *élan* will overcome the enemy's will to fight. The moral is everything, the material nothing."

This philosophy was eventually officially adopted in the 1913 Field Regulations, containing the Eight Commandments of Offensive Warfare. The Regulations, which were intended to be a general guide for tactical training, were fruity with phrases like "offensive without hesitation", "fierceness and tenacity", and so on. Evidently, the Regulations did not take into account the effects of shrapnel and machine guns on men in the open field. Experience in combat was showing that, on the battlefield, *élan* was not proof against a 7.7-centimeter shell, and the offensive spirit could not deflect machine gun bullets.

Actually, Grandmaison was not the originator of this tactical approach; he was teaching a much abridged version of theories developed by Ferdinand Foch. The portion of Foch's ideas that Grandmaison left out of his lectures was the most important part, in Hughes' estimation: Foch's emphasis on the importance of preparation, planning, security, what Foch termed *sureté*. The thought reminded Hughes that Foch was nearby, in command of the 20th Corps which was supposed to be attacking somewhere south of Morhange. He wondered

49

if the 20th was having any better luck with their assignment than the 15th Corps was here. He returned to 15th Corps Headquarters to consult with General Gerard again.

"You saw for yourself, then?" Gerard asked Hughes. "This has been going on for the last two days, and our casualties, especially among the junior officers and veteran non-coms have been so heavy that many of the units have lost cohesion. That is why I told General deCastlenau that I do not believe this Corps will be capable of further offensive operations without substantial reinforcements, heavy artillery support and at least 48 hours to reorganize some of the most badly mangled units. In fact, in its current condition, I am far from certain that the Corps can hold this position in the event of a German counter-attack."

Major Hughes did not venture to argue the point. The Second Army was continuing to pressure the corps commanders, because General Joffre in Paris was putting the Second Army's commander's feet to the fire (and probably those of all of the other army commanders as well), demanding that they attack and break through the German positions. Major Hughes was sure that General deCastlenau was not interested in hearing excuses as to why the assignment could not be carried out, any more than General Joffre in GHQ wanted to hear why Second Army was not taking its assigned objectives. In any event, both the Commander-in-Chief and the commanding general of the Second Army were ardent believers in the *offensive à outrance*. Hughes did not think there was the slightest possibility that the 15th Corps would be able to carry the German positions on their front, but Plan XVII required it to do so. The situation was a disaster waiting to happen.

And sure enough, disaster, in the form of a heavy German counter-attack, struck the weakened and demoralized 15th Corps that very afternoon.

Through his field glasses, Hughes looked upon a scene out of a nightmare. French soldiers in their blue jackets and red pants ran towards him in a disorganized mob. Discarded packs littered the ground, and many of the men had cast away their rifles and were unarmed. German shells landing among the fleeing *poilus* blasted some to bloody fragments as they ran to the rear. Some wounded men limped along with improvised crutches, while others were carried by their mates. Artillerymen frantically whipped the horses pulling the gun carriages, urging them on to greater speed. Hughes saw numerous dead soldiers lying crumpled on the ground, arms out-flung in bizarre attitudes of death. A few small groups of *poilus* here and there still had some fight left in them. They crouched behind some bit of cover, firing their rifles in the direction of the enemy and standing their ground. But there were not enough of them. Most of the 15th Corps had seen enough fighting for today, and the Corps was melting away before his eyes.

As he watched, he described what he saw on a field telephone to General deCastlenau himself, at Second Army Headquarters. The General asked Hughes a question. "The *boche* artillery was pounding them, General," he replied. "As you know, their field pieces outrange our 75s. The artillery bombardment went on for about two hours, causing very heavy casualties, as the Corp's position had no natural cover and the men were not dug in..." (because they had been taught that the French soldier never digs in, he only attacks, Hughes thought) "...and then they were taken by a surprise attack in the flank from a forest... a moment please, General..." Hughes fumbled with a map, finally succeeding in unfolding it to the right section. "...the Forest of Bride and Koeking, about three kilometers east of here."

Another question came from the commanding General of the Second Army. "General, I do not believe that these men will be able to rally this side of Nancy, but they may be able to fight again, if they get behind our fortress line. In the meantime, may I suggest that if we do not get some reinforcements to plug this hole in our line, the *boches* may be in Nancy before our men are?"

After Hughes returned to Headquarters, he quickly went through the reports from the entire Second Army. The French offensive had been everywhere either driven back by German counter-attacks, or forced to retreat to avoid being surrounded when a neighboring unit was defeated. The next day he discovered that the same story had been repeated up and down the line: all the French armies, from the Swiss border to Luxembourg, had been repulsed with heavy losses. Plan XVII was an unmitigated calamity.

Hughes had heard that the Russians had surprised everyone by launching an offensive in East Prussia before anybody thought they could be ready. He wondered how they were doing. Better than us, I hope, he thought. If not, the war may be lost almost before it has begun.

Chapter Five: East Prussia, August 21, 1914

In the slanting sunlight of late afternoon, Ray Swing peered through his field glasses at the Russian positions in the little village of Bischofstien, perhaps a mile away. Beside him in the stone barn, Lieutenant-Colonel Max Hoffman of the German 8th Army was also surveying the hastily prepared earthworks the defenders had thrown up.

Hoffman had been posted as a military observer attached to the Japanese Army during the Russo-Japanese War, and was therefore considered something of Russian specialist in the German Army. He had learned respect for the phenomenal courage and endurance of the Russian soldier. On the other hand, he had nothing but contempt for the officers who led them. He shared with Swing his opinion that the Russians were particularly incompetent in the area of logistics, describing two occasions when he saw the Japanese overrun Russian positions after the defenders ran out of ammunition.

"The typical Russian officer is brave, has some understanding of platoon-level tactics and can sit a horse well," Hoffman said. "Beyond that, he understands practically nothing about modern warfare, and that describes most of their officer corps right up to their General Staff, as far as I am aware."

The two men were waiting for a German assault to begin, the day's second attempt to take this key crossroads and complete the encirclement of the Russian Second Army.

They had witnessed the first try, earlier in the day. The German artillery had pounded the Russian trenches heavily for a half hour. Shells screamed overhead, blasting great fountains of dirt, mud, wood and pieces of unidentifiable objects into the air. Several of the houses in the little village were knocked down, and many of the wood-shingled roofs were on fire or at least smoldering.

Swing, who had never before witnessed combat, thought the violence of the bombardment was impressively terrifying. He found it hard to believe that anyone was still alive in the Russian trenches after the barrage. When the shelling let up, he was about to ask Hoffman his opinion, but before he could, the German was already answering the unasked question.

"Not enough, not enough," he muttered without taking the binoculars from his eyes. "That is not going to do it. Raymond, if you want to see what modern small arms can do on the battlefield, watch closely," he said.

Whistles blew, and the German assault troops emerged from behind the trees and buildings where they had gathered prior to the assault. They moved forward across the potato fields in dense bunches, their rifles pointing forward at the enemy, their bayonets fixed. The Russians began to fire, a faint crackling sound, and the Germans began to fall, at first a few at a time, then many more in rapid succession. Swing could hear the cries of the wounded men as the attack moved forward.

Now, there came a new sound, a deep chattering noise. "That would be the 1910 Maxim," Hoffman said. "Effective range is around 1000 meters, at a rate of 600 rounds a minute." As he spoke, Swing saw the Russian machine gun cut swathes in the lines of gray-clad soldiers. Before a single German had reached the Russian lines, the attack had faltered, the soldiers flinging themselves to the ground just to stay alive. The whistles blew again, and the Germans went back to the jumping-off points, carrying dead and wounded comrades.

"Terrible," commented Hoffman. "Completely inadequate artillery preparation. The position must be bombarded for twice as long as that, to break up their earthworks and neutralize those machine gun nests." He pulled his watch from his pocket, and said, "There is time to organize one more assault today. With more thorough artillery preparation, it can be done."

They settled down to wait.

*

Ray Swing had spent considerable time and money cultivating potential sources since his assignment to Berlin. An experienced British reporter he met shortly after arriving in Germany had suggested that if he wanted good inside information on the German Army, he could do worse than getting to know Lieutenant-Colonel Max Hoffman. Swing had taken the reporter's advice, spending several moderately expensive evenings buying drinks for Hoffman (the Lieutenant-Colonel favored French cognac), and becoming friendly with the man. As soon as war was declared, Swing called Hoffman to see if some strings could be pulled that would get him to the front. As it happened, Hoffman himself was available to take Swing out to the battlefield.

The 41 year old Hoffman was tall and burly, with close-cropped hair on a large head. He was intelligent, knowledgeable and helpful to his friends, of which Swing was glad to include himself. He had served in the Russian section of the General Staff before the war, and then been posted to 8th Army in East Prussia where he was General Prittwitz's deputy chief of staff. The 8th's assignment was to defend East Prussia in the unlikely event that the Russians were able to launch an offensive there before the Schlieffen Plan had crushed the French and released the armies committed in the West. That all changed when orders from Berlin cancelled the Schlieffen Plan, called off the invasion of Belgium, and sent 750,000 men of the 1st, 2nd, 3rd and 4th Armies that were originally intended to march west to East Prussia instead.

The 8th Army was placed in reserve, while General Moltke himself directed a hastily devised campaign against the Russians, using the field armies that had been shipped in from the west. Under the circumstances, Hoffman found himself with time on his hands. When Swing approached him, he readily obtained permission to go on detached duty to conduct the American reporter around the battlefields ("To keep him out of trouble" was the way Hoffman described it to General Prittwitz.)

As they rode the train to Marienburg, the end of the line in East Prussia, Hoffman filled Swing in on the military situation.

"As it turned out, it was fortunate for us that the invasion of Belgium was called off," Hoffman explained. "The Russians weren't supposed to be able to organize anything bigger than a cavalry raid for two months after the war started, but somehow they were able to deliver two field armies to the border and send them into East Prussia in less than two *weeks*. We estimate that they have about 600,000 men altogether." He shook his head at the thought. "I *still* do not see how they were able to bring up enough ammunition for that many men, even leaving aside the question of rations." He paused, as if calculating something, and then went on. "The Eighth Army had a total of perhaps 135,000 men to stop them."

"That's more than four to one in their favor," Swing said. "But, with the new German troops coming from the west…"

Hoffman nodded, "The balance tilts back in our favor. Heavily in our favor, I would say. There is a question of quality, after all. For example, consider artillery." His voice took on an authoritative ring, as if he was delivering a report to the General Staff. "We have both more guns and superior ones, as well as better trained crews. Just based on that advantage alone, the combat efficiency of a German division is probably half again that of a Russian one. Also, the Russians will certainly have serious logistical issues. They will be operating far from their nearest railheads, and their wagon train is completely inadequate to supply such large armies. As for their leadership... let us just say that the Russian officer corps is not trained to German standards." He shook his head again.

"Objectively, I would rate the fighting power of a German division at twice that of a Russian one," Hoffman concluded. "So you see, we really outnumber them in effective combat strength by at least two to one."

Swing had been scribbling furiously while the German spoke. "Would it be fair to say that you are confident the Russian armies will be driven off German soil?" Swing asked, his pencil poised over his notepad.

Colonel Hoffman's lips curled upward in a grin, which could only be described as "carnivorous". "No, Raymond, I do not expect the Russian armies to be 'driven off' German soil," he answered. "I expect them to be annihilated."

In Marienburg, Hoffman took Swing to 8th Army headquarters and introduced him to his commanding officer, General Prittwitz, and another general with the oddly Gallic name of Francois. That the 8th Army had not been given an active role in the German plan disgusted Prittwitz and his staff. Swing discovered that Hoffman's colleagues on the 8th Army staff were as surprised as he that the despised Russians had managed to organize an invasion so quickly, and that they were equally as confident that the Czar's soldiers would soon be obliterated.

Hoffman asked for a copy of Moltke's orders, then for a map of the planned offensive. He studied the materials closely for a few minutes, pulled his watch from his pocket and glanced at it, then stabbed the map decisively with a thick finger.

"We will go over to Bischofstien," he told Swing. "The Twentieth Corps will be assaulting the town this afternoon." Hoffman ordered a staff car and driver, and they were bumping down a dirt road through the Prussian countryside a few minutes later.

Hoffman used his fertile imagination to get them to an artillery O.P. in a stone barn near the starting line for the attack. Swing's German was far from perfect, but it sounded to him as if Hoffman claimed that *Oberstgeneral* Moltke himself had authorized him to bring the American correspondent with him up to this advanced post almost at the front line. He was not one hundred percent sure, but he thought he heard Hoffman tell a skeptical artillery Major named Bruckner that Swing was a nephew of President Wilson.

*

The assault on Bischofstien was renewed three hours later, beginning with an artillery barrage that made the one Swing had witnessed earlier in the day seem positively feeble by comparison. The Germans were evidently using both more guns and larger caliber ones as well. *This* bombardment did not stop after a mere thirty minutes, but instead went on for an hour and a half.

The effect of the second shelling on the Russian works was almost indescribable. Swing saw blasts fling brown clad soldiers out of their shallow entrenchments like rag dolls, machine gun nests and their crews buried under mountains of loose earth. His field glasses showed a scene of hell on earth, with trees knocked flat, houses blown to pieces, horses gone mad with fear running wildly across no-mans-land and dead men lying everywhere. The wooden, thatch-roofed houses that made up the little farming village of Bischofstien, most of which had survived the morning assault reasonably intact, were reduced a pile of flaming rubble. A light eastern wind carried wisps of smoke and the sharp smell of cordite to the German lines.

When silence finally fell, Hoffman nodded approvingly. Through the ringing in his ears, Swing heard the German say, "*That* should do it."

He dimly heard whistles blowing, and thousands of voices shouting. Once again, from out of the woods on either side and in front of the barn jogged masses of gray-clad soldiers. As they moved across the open field toward the town, Swing heard the crack of rifle fire and saw orange muzzle flashes from the Russian trenches. He was amazed to see that even this heavy shelling had not killed or incapacitated all of the defenders.

Swing could tell from the sound that this time there were many fewer rifles firing, and no Maxim guns in action at all. Some of the Germans were felled by the defenders' fire, but not enough of them to even slow the down the momentum of the assault. It was clear that there simply were not enough Russian riflemen left to hold the position in front of village. In just a few minutes, the German assault was across the fields and in the town, overrunning the Russian positions, shooting the defenders at close range, or spearing them with their bayonets. Swing was surprised that the Russians did not surrender, even when it became obvious that continued defense was hopeless.

Hoffman was thinking along the same lines. "Brave bastards, aren't they?" he commented. He lowered his binoculars. "Give them a few more minutes and then we can go into the town behind them, if you want a look at the Russian positions."

Swing fought to keep his lunch down as he inspected the mutilated bodies and parts of bodies in the formerly Russian trenches. There were only so many corpses that he could look at before he had seen his fill. Hoffman was inspecting the Russian dead thoughtfully.

"Just look at how few rifles are here," he said, sweeping his arm to indicate a section of earthworks containing perhaps twenty dead Russians. "I see no more than six. I wonder..." He set off rapidly, surveying another section of the field works, Swing at his heels.

"You know," he said at last, "I do not believe they had weapons for more than half of their men, perhaps not even for that many. How were they supposed to fight without rifles, I wonder?" He shook his head at the thought.

"We can go back to Marienburg now, and tomorrow we will return to see the Russians surrender, I think," Hoffman told Swing.

As they trudged across the shell-torn field back to the staff car, Swing asked, "Surrender? How can you be so sure?"

"The road through Bischofstien was the last connection their Second Army had back to their supply train," Hoffman explained. "After two days of fighting, they are almost certainly either out or nearly out of food, small-arms and artillery ammunition, and everything else. Also, their communications are cut to pieces, so headquarters is no longer in control of their men. By tomorrow afternoon, there will no longer be a Russian army here, only a leaderless mob."

That night, after he had finished writing his story, he paused to wonder again who had made the decision to cancel the invasion of Belgium, and why. Whatever the reason, it looked as if it had been the right one for Germany. This as yet unnamed great victory in East Prussia was only the beginning, he suspected. The gray tide of the German Army was flowing strongly into the East, and Russia was about to be engulfed in it.

Chapter Six: East Prussia, August 25, 1914

As First Lieutenant Joseph Stilwell listened to his host, he experienced a mix of amusement and irritation, although he made sure not to allow either emotion show on his face. Captain Ernst von Luettner had done nothing to deserve either, and especially not anything that could be interpreted as dissatisfaction. On the contrary, the man had gone out of his way to be helpful.

The source of his amusement was the great variance between the German's appearance and his speech.

Von Luettner could have served as the model for a painting entitled "The Prussian Military Beast." He had the requisite ramrod stiff posture, the Iron Cross (second class) pinned to his chest, dueling scar on his cheek below the left eye (from Heidelberg, no doubt), the Kaiser-inspired, upturned, waxed, spiked mustache, and even the obligatory monocle dangling from a silver chain on his chest. One look at him, and you knew that he would speak with the arrogant bark of the Prussian military aristocracy, and his English, if he bothered to learn it at all, would have the sharp Teutonic accents of his class.

So when this prototype Junker introduced himself, Stilwell was forced to suppress a smile when out of Luettner's mouth came a pure upper crust Oxbridge English accent with a speech pattern to match. Even after spending half a day in the Captain's company, Stilwell found that if he closed his eyes when the German was speaking, he could imagine he was listening to the Duke of Bedfordshire, the Earl of Southampton or some other twig from the tree of the British aristocracy. There was an explanation, of course. The loquacious Luettner volunteered almost as soon as they met that he had attended Oxford for four years on a Rhodes scholarship.

What the German did not know, and Stilwell had no intention of allowing him to find out, was that the American military attaché nurtured a deep, abiding and (he had to admit it to himself), almost irrational antipathy for the British, especially for the upper classes. The accent had an effect on Stilwell that was not unlike fingernails scraping a blackboard, which accounted for the irritation.

Under the circumstances, Stilwell was on his best behavior, as he did not want to risk offending the man who was now taking him out to observe the German Army in action against the Russians. Ambassador Gerard had stressed that his bosses in Washington had been putting on pressure to provide reliable eyewitness reports on the fighting in the East from someone other than a newspaper reporter. Stilwell had other orders as well, these from the War Department, which required him to provide detailed reports on the strengths and weaknesses of the Kaiser's army in action against the Russians. The cooperative Captain Luettner had thus far done everything Stilwell needed to carry out his assignments.

The East Prussian countryside was mostly flat, and the scenery consisted mostly of pine forests alternating with farms and swamps. As they drove in the big staff car down the rutted dirt road accompanied by clouds of dust, Luettner pointed out what Stilwell estimated to be at least twenty thousand men in brown uniforms, sitting or wandering aimlessly around a cow pasture surrounded by some hastily-erected barbed-wire fences. From nearby came the sounds of hammers and saws. Stilwell could see the beginnings of simple wooden buildings and tall guard towers being constructed on a fallow field.

"These chaps are some of the prisoners we took from the Russian Second Army in the Battles of East Prussia." This was the name given to the recently concluded four-day battle that had extended over hundreds of kilometers which had resulted, according to German dispatches, in the near-total destruction of two Russian field armies.

"We're setting them to work building some of those, what do the English call them... ah, 'concentration camps'," Luettner shouted over the roar of the automobile engine.

As it happened, Stilwell was familiar with concentration camps. He had seen them in the Philippines in 1904, during his service in the Philippine Insurrection. The United States Army had found it impossible to contain Aguinaldo's hit-and-run guerilla tactics with conventional warfare, so they simply rounded up the civilian population that supported the guerrillas and locked them up. Camps were quickly constructed by stringing barbed wire on wooden posts to create an enclosure and putting up few guard towers with machine guns to produce a cheap, effective prison.

"I am told that these fellows fought like the very devil, even after they were surrounded," Luettner went on. "Most of them only surrendered when they completely ran out of ammunition."

"Is it true that only half of their men had rifles when they went into action?" Stilwell yelled, clutching a door handle with one hand and the old Philippine Insurrection campaign hat that he invariably wore in the field with the other, as the car bounced through a huge pothole.

"That is what the battlefield reports say," the German captain agreed. "Fancy sending your chaps out to fight without weapons! Apparently, the ones without rifles were expected to follow those who had them, and arm themselves from the casualties." He shook his head. "Not that it would have done them much good if they had weapons. There wasn't enough ammunition for the ones they did have."

As they drove, they passed long lines of gray-clad German soldiers marching through the dust toward the front accompanied by big cook wagons pulled by mules, and by caissons and horse-drawn field pieces. The soldiers waved and shouted greetings as the big staff car roared by.

Luettner pointed to a stand of woods across a field. "The commander of the Russian Second Army, a chap named Samsonov, I believe, shot himself over in that copse of trees after the battle."

Stilwell shouted another question. "I also heard that the Russians sent out their orders on the wireless in clear. That can't be right, can it?" Stilwell had gotten this story from Ray Swing after the latter had returned from his trip to the front. Swing had been unable to confirm the truth of the story, and a skeptical Stilwell had voiced doubts that even the Czar's generals could be *that* stupid.

Luettner smiled and nodded his head. "At first, when our chaps picked up Ivan's orders from the air, Intelligence thought it must be some sort of clever ruse. But then we saw that the Russian units were making precisely the movements ordered by the intercepted transmissions, so we knew they were the genuine article. The damned odd thing is that they had codes and codebooks. They simply didn't use them."

German morale seemed to be high, Stilwell observed. Many of the men were singing or laughing as they moved east on the dusty roads. Well, why not? Stilwell thought. It's a lot more fun when you're winning.

"How many prisoners did you end up taking altogether?" he asked.

The German shook his head. "Sorry, old boy. Can't tell you that."

Stilwell nodded with a certain grim satisfaction. The Germans had been a little *too* cooperative with the American military observer. Suspicious by nature, Stilwell had assumed that eventually he would ask a question that they were not going to answer.

"Military secret, I suppose," he grunted.

Captain Luettner looked at Stilwell in surprise and began to laugh. "Hardly that, old chap. We simply haven't finished counting them all. Intelligence estimates that we bagged most of the First and Second Russian field armies in the battle here. We've counted 500,000 so far."

Luettner chuckled. "What was it that your General Sherman said? 'They have fought their last man, and even *he* is running?' Quite well put, that."

"It was Longstreet, at Chickamauga," Stilwell replied tonelessly. He was stunned by the scope of the German victory. Half a million prisoners taken in one battle? It was almost unbelievable, yet everything about Luettner's manner indicated that the man was telling him nothing but the unvarnished truth. Stilwell wondered if the Russians could halt the Germans this side of Moscow after such a catastrophe. It also occurred to him that the United States had better not get involved in a war with Germany anytime soon; the U.S. Army as presently constituted was a long way from being ready to take on *this* foe.

Luettner turned right off the main road and onto a narrow side road that ran up a hill to the right. The road was bordered by a thick growth of pines and underbrush that was impenetrable to the eye.

"Say, I thought we were going to observe a river crossing," Stilwell protested. "The front's that way, isn't it?" he asked, pointing east, the direction they had been traveling.

The German smiled. "And we shall get an excellent view of it from up on this hill. I have orders not to allow you to get too close to the fighting. Imagine the fuss if you were killed! The French newspapers would be screaming tomorrow that the *boches* had assassinated the American military attaché. My dear fellow, you must see that that wouldn't do at all."

Stilwell could see the logic in this, but he still wanted to get closer to the action. "I know for a fact that you let the newspaper boys get closer than this," he grumbled.

"Ah, but news reporters are not official representatives of the American government, are they?" Luettner asked. "You can see, I think, how that would make a difference, at least from my government's point of view."

Seeing that it was pointless to argue, Stilwell reluctantly subsided.

Luettner pulled the car off the road and into a small clearing. There was an opening in the foliage in the direction of the front, and Stilwell could see that the hill's elevation gave them an excellent view of miles of the East Prussian countryside spread out below.

"Never fear, old man," said Luettner, as he went into the trunk of the car and pulled out some black metal poles that proved to be a tripod stand. He set up the stand, went back to the trunk and brought out an enormous pair of periscope-style German field glasses, which he secured to the stand with a screw.

"There you are," he said, gesturing at the field glasses. "You'll have a better view of the crossing operation than the divisional commander himself."

From up on the elevation Stilwell could now hear the distant thumps of the German artillery pounding the Russian positions on the other side of the not very wide river.

"That's the Niemen River over there," volunteered Luettner, now peering through another, smaller pair of glasses, before Stilwell could ask. "You can see what's left of the old bridge over on the left. Ivan demolished it yesterday when he retreated through here."

Stilwell could see the ruins of a small suspension bridge whose main span formed a downward angle, with the vertex collapsed in the river.

"Some of General Kluck's lads will be putting in the attack," Luettner continued. "It looks as if we got here just in time for the show."

Stilwell turned his glasses on the Russian positions. He was unimpressed by what he saw of the defensive preparations. The shallow trenches occupied by the infantry afforded almost no protection from the heavy German shelling. There was no counter-battery fire from the Russian artillery. The latter seemed to have very few guns of their own (mostly French 75s, according to information Stilwell had been given), and these few were out-ranged by the heavier German howitzers and other field guns. He speculated that most of Russian field pieces had probably been lost in the disaster two days earlier.

As he watched, the remaining Russian batteries began limbering up the guns, harnessing the horses and pulling out. They were not leaving any too soon. He saw a German shell explode in the midst of one of the Russian batteries, dismounting two guns and knocking over several men who served them.

He surveyed the near bank of the Niemen. The wind carried the faint popping sounds of the German rifle and machine gun fire and the feeble Russian response up to the hill. Masses of the gray-clad Germans were pouring heavy small arms fire on the Russians about a quarter-mile away from them on the opposite side of the river.

He now saw groups of soldiers rushing from out of the pines near the river, carrying boats. Stilwell estimated that the boats were about 15 feet long. Each one was being carried by eight men. They swarmed into the water, leaping into the boats and paddling furiously across the river under Russian fire. One or two soldiers in each boat were shooting back at the far bank as their fellows propelled the assault craft.

The Russian fire seemed to have little effect on the attackers. Stilwell judged that the heavy volleys of small arms fire from the German side of the river combined with shelling by the German artillery had effectively suppressed the defenders' counter-fire. In what seemed like only a few moments, the German boats were beaching on the far bank, and the assault troops were scrambling out of the boats and moving on the Russian positions.

A Russian officer on horseback appeared, waving his sword over his head and trotting back and forth behind the infantry, trying to encourage his men, and making himself a huge target for the German riflemen. The American estimated the officer's life expectancy at about twenty seconds and, sure enough, almost immediately he and his horse were knocked down by German sharpshooters. A man on horseback was just too big a target on the modern battlefield, where the infantry was universally armed with rifles with effective ranges of nearly a mile. Every army on Earth should have learned that lesson from the American Civil War, but evidently the word had not yet reached some members of the Russian officer corps.

"There's brave and then there's just plain stupid," he muttered to himself. How could an officer lead his men if he was a casualty? he asked himself. You had to risk your neck sometimes, sure, but in this case the Russian officer had sacrificed his life for nothing, and now there was no one left to lead the defense of the position or to organize an orderly withdrawal, which was soon going to be necessary. His men were left to their own devices.

The Russians were already wavering before their gallant but foolhardy officer was killed. Soon, the brown-clad defenders began emerging from their earthworks, waving white rags tied on the ends of sticks or rifles, throwing down their weapons and putting their hands in the air. Others further back were abandoning their shallow trenches and running into the woods behind the position.

"*These* fellows aren't exactly fighting to the last man, are they Captain?" Stilwell commented, watching the rout.

"Perhaps their morale is not quite what it was a few days ago," the German suggested. "Then too, they very likely had their best men in the frontline divisions, and most of them were captured or killed, so what remains may not be ..." he hesitated.

"Not their first team, shall we say?" Stilwell finished for him.

"Ah, they're bringing up the pontoons," Luettner said, pointing.

Stilwell saw a line of trucks pull up to a low point on the riverbank near the ruined bridge. The Germans began sliding out the pontoons, which looked like long, flat-prowed fishing boats, from the backs of the trucks and dragging them down to the river. As he watched, the pontoons were drawn into the Niemen and rapidly connected together with ropes or cables (he could not see which) side by side, creating a line of floats extending out into the river. In almost no time, the bridge of boats had reached the opposite bank of the river, and soldiers on the near side began laying wooden planks over the top to create a walkway. They were followed by engineers who secured the planks to the pontoons and to neighboring planks. Almost before the last piece of wood was secured in place on the far side of the Niemen, columns of spike-helmeted soldiers were marching across the newly completed bridge. Stilwell pulled his watch from his pocket and stared at it. The whole operation, he saw, from the initial river crossing to a defended far bank, to the completion of the pontoon bridge, had only taken two hours.

"I trust you've seen enough for your report, Lieutenant Stilwell," Luettner said. "Suppose we pop over to First Army Headquarters and I introduce you to General von Kluck. I should think that he would want to hear your impressions of the river crossing operation."

As they drove away, Stilwell reflected that unless the Russian Army could put up a better fight than they had done so far in East Prussia, they might discover that the war with Germany was over almost before it began.

Chapter Seven: Off Tunisia, September 2, 1914

Sub-Lieutenant King-Hall heard the distant thump of guns while he was still at breakfast. He immediately dropped a fork still bearing a piece of fried sausage to clatter on his plate, and rose, gulping down a last mouthful of egg.

Snatching his hat from the table, he left the officer's mess and rushed out into the passageway, before he remembered being told as a cadet back at the Royal Naval College that "an officer should always give the men an impression of calm, most particularly when he is excited himself." He took a deep breath, settled his hat on his head, and walked in what he thought of as a measured but expedient pace to his duty station as junior watch officer on the bridge of the HMS *Southampton*, lately of the Royal Navy's First Light Cruiser Squadron of the Grand Fleet, now on detached duty with the Mediterranean Fleet. This was the 21-year-old King-Hall's first shipboard assignment, and he was eager, not to say anxious, to do well in it. King-Hall's family had a long tradition of service in the Royal Navy, which created high expectations for him. He was certain that his father, Admiral Sir George Fowler King-Hall, was reading his son's fitness reports almost as soon as they were filed.

Considering everything, it was not surprising that his pace was more expedient than measured, so that when he reached the bridge after rapidly ascending the ladders from two decks below, the young Sub-Lieutenant found that he was breathing a little harder than he would have liked.

Commodore Tyrwhitt, commander of the light cruiser squadron, was on the bridge already, talking to the *Southampton*'s skipper, Captain Goodenough. Tyrwhitt smiled at King-Hall as the latter saluted the squadron's commanding officer and announced a trifle breathlessly, "Sub-Lieutenant King-Hall reporting for duty, sir."

"If you were worried that you would be late, Mr. King-Hall, I have good news for you," said Tyrwhitt, returning the salute and consulting his watch. "You are in fact early, by six minutes to be precise." Captain Goodenough and the ship's Executive Officer, Lieutenant Commander Summers allowed themselves a brief grin before returning to their duties.

This was almost a standing joke between the Commodore and his most junior officer. Since he had come aboard *Southampton* in February a day earlier than required by his orders, King-Hall had reported early for duty every day without exception.

"Yes, sir," King-Hall replied. The joke was really one-sided. The young Sub-Lieutenant saw nothing particularly amusing about being prompt for duty. "I thought I heard some shooting while I was having breakfast."

Lieutenant-Commander Summers was peering out to sea at the Allied fleet. He responded without lowering his binoculars. "It seems that the French commander here is looking for a fight," he said. "Souchon sent the usual torpedo boat with the parley flag to the port, but before it could get near the harbor, someone in the old fort put two shots across its bow and the boat turned back."

Southampton and her two sister light cruisers had been shadowing the Allied German-Austrian-Italian squadron around the western Mediterranean for the better part of a month. The Allied fleet, under the command of German Admiral Wilhelm Souchon, was led by Souchon's flagship, the battlecruiser *Goeben*, reputedly able to sink anything in the French Navy all by herself. *Goeben* was armed with a main battery of ten 11-inch Krupp naval rifles, and was rumored to be capable of an astonishing 28-knot top speed. Keeping

Goeben company were three Austrian dreadnoughts of the *Tegettoff* class: *Prinz Eugen*, *Viribus Unitis* and *Tegettoff* herself, all with 12-inch main batteries, and flank speeds greater than twenty knots, and three *Cavour* class dreadnoughts contributed by the Italian *Regia Marina*, each with thirteen 12-inch guns and protected by 10-inch armor belts.

This powerful force was escorted by numerous cruisers, destroyers, torpedo boats and other auxiliaries. Souchon's fleet had cruised along the coast of French North Africa as if it had taken a mortgage on the place, sailing from one French colonial port to another. Another, even more powerful fleet, composed entirely of German ships of the High Seas Fleet, and operating out of Genoa, the nearest major port of Germany's Italian ally, under the command of Admiral Reinhard Scheer, patrolled the northern side of the Mediterranean, keeping the main French battle fleet penned up in their home port of Toulon. The Allied and German ships were re-fueled by colliers out of Sicily and Sardinia, and used Italian ports for re-fitting and repairs as needed.

These Triple Alliance fleets were free to go wherever they wished in the Mediterranean and elsewhere without the slightest concern for what the Royal Navy might do. A neutral Great Britain had allowed Germany and her allies to dominate the much smaller French Navy both here and along France's Atlantic ports. The latter, from Dunkirk on the English Channel all the way to Bayonne on the Bay of Biscay, were already cut off from the outside world by blockading German destroyers and cruisers, just as the southern ports were interdicted by the massive squadrons under Scheer and Souchon.

At each North African port visited by the Souchon's fleet thus far, events had followed an unvarying pattern. First, the German Admiral would send a torpedo boat under a flag of truce into the harbor. All ships in the port were ordered to come out within a short time limit,

73

usually six hours. Then, when the ships emerged under the guns of the Allied battleships, they were boarded by sailors from Souchon's destroyers and cruisers. Neutral vessels were sent on their various ways, while French merchantmen were seized and taken by Allied prize crews to Italian, Austrian or German ports and the original crews were put ashore. After the harbor had been cleared of shipping, the Allied ships would bombard the defenseless port, destroying warehouses, wharves, dry docks and any other facilities that might be used for commerce, leaving behind burning ruins. The few French warships that had been trapped in the ports had not offered to challenge the Allied fleet's overwhelming firepower, but had been scuttled by their skippers to keep them from falling into the hands of the Germans.

King-Hall was uncomfortable with his assignment on the *Southampton*, although he gave no outward sign of it. His unease was not caused by the weather, the ship or his fellow officers. The warm, calm Mediterranean Sea was certainly a pleasant change from the gales and icy winds of the Atlantic and the Channel. The *Southampton* was a fine ship, one of the most modern in the Royal Navy, well designed and maintained. His superior officers were amazingly easy to get on with (at least compared to the instructors at the Royal Naval College!), and impressively knowledgeable, competent and efficient. He considered himself very lucky to be able to serve under Commodore Tyrwhitt, who was widely considered one of the most brilliant young officers in the R.N., and a sure bet to be called up to the Admiralty soon. He could not even honestly say that the assignment itself was uninteresting.

What bothered King-Hall was the feeling that the Royal Navy and England should be doing more than watching Souchon and his fleet dismantle the French North African ports. He felt that they should be *helping*

74

the French, not just standing by to see them get pummeled into submission.

In any case, here in Tunis it seemed that the pattern was about to be broken. Here, the French commander was not going to give up without challenging the powerful Allied fleet.

"What sort of information do we have on the French naval forces based in Tunis, Mr. King-Hall?" asked Commodore Tyrwhitt.

The young officer pulled a notebook from a chart rack attached to the bulkhead. This book contained Naval Intelligence information on the naval strengths of the various Mediterranean Sea powers, from Spain in the west to Russia in the northeast.

King-Hall paged through the book until he came to the entry for Tunis.

"They have a squadron stationed here under Rear Admiral Emile DuPay. There are two armored cruisers of the *Edgar Quinet* class: the *Waldeck-Rousseau* and the *Edgar Quinet* herself, with fourteen 7 ½ inch guns, rated at 23 knots…"

"When were the *Quinets* put in service, around 1910 or 1911?" interrupted Lieutenant-Commander Summers.

"That's right, sir," responded King-Hall, still scanning the report, "1911 to be exact."

"Obsolete design, out of date before they were launched," was Tyrwhitt's comment. "What else have they got?"

"Just a destroyer squadron, sir" the Sub-Lieutenant answered. "Five of them, *Spahi* class, launched between 1908 and 1911, with six…" he hesitated: "…can this be right? It says they have six-gun, 6.5 centimeter main batteries? That's only two and a half inches. Can they mean to send their men out to fight the German battleships with those popguns, sir?" King-Hall asked, appalled at the thought.

75

"Evidently," replied the Commodore. He fished a pipe from his pocket, stuffed it with a wad of shag from a leather pouch, then struck a match and lit up. "Keep in mind that our own destroyers only have four inch guns, which would not be significantly better in this kind of battle, against capital ships. A destroyer's principal weapons against larger ships are its torpedoes, not its guns. The difficulty for the destroyer, of course, is getting within effective range to use the torpedoes before being sunk by gunfire."

Summers was still peering at the harbor entrance through his field glasses. "They're coming out," he announced.

In another moment they could all see black columns of smoke rising into the blue Mediterranean sky over the entrance to the harbor, as the French squadron left Tunis and gallantly steamed out to attack the Allied fleet. The French used high-sulfur coal to fuel their ships, producing particularly black clouds of exhaust that could be seen from a long distance.

Through his binoculars, King-Hall could see the French ships emerging in single file, with the destroyers in the van, followed by the armored cruisers. The Rear Admiral's flag flew from the first cruiser to clear the harbor. Evidently, Admiral DuPay intended to conduct this battle in person.

"Brave chap there," commented Tyrwhitt.

It was a bit of hard luck for his men though, King-Hall thought. And what would it prove if DuPay's courage ended by losing all his ships and men in this suicidal attack? It certainly would not help his country win the war.

As the last French ship cleared the harbor entrance, King-Hall saw the orange winks of the muzzle flashes from the Allied big guns and seconds later heard the booms of the eleven- and twelve-inch main batteries. The Allied ships were still far out of the maximum range for the armored cruisers' main batteries, when great fountaining splashes thrown up by misses from the big shells began to straddle the doomed French squadron.

King-Hall was not especially impressed by the accuracy of the Allied fire, in spite of its overwhelming volume. The first salvo did not score any hits, but the Frenchmen's good fortune did not continue for very long. He saw two of the low, narrow destroyers hit by large-caliber shells. The first destroyer was struck amidships, at the base of the bridge. The bridge was enveloped in a fireball, then the ship careened out of formation and drifted to a dead stop, burning from stem to stern.

The end of the second destroyer was more spectacular. There was an immense blast and a huge, hellish ball of smoke and flame rose over the sea. When the black cloud drifted away, the destroyer was gone, vanished. Only a few bits of flotsam drifted on the water where there had been a live ship seconds earlier.

King-Hall saw the muzzle flashes from the guns of the French armored cruisers trying to strike back at their tormentors. They were still hopelessly out of range: the splashes of their shells were at least a two hundred yards short of the nearest Allied ships.

Now the Allied dreadnoughts began to find the range of the French armored cruisers. The lead cruiser, flying the Admiral's flag, was hit three times in rapid succession. The third shell knocked off the French flagship's bow and she slowed to a dead stop. At that point, the stationary armored cruiser became a floating target for an avalanche of shellfire. After she was hit four more times, the cruiser's stern lifted high in the air and she sank by the bow in less than a minute.

All the remaining French ships were now on fire, with the exception of one destroyer which seemed to enjoy a charmed life. Huge waterspouts of near misses repeatedly straddled the little ship, but somehow she continued on undamaged. Moreover, Admiral Souchon had been careless in the deployment of his overwhelming force, and the French destroyer had somehow cleared the Allied picket line and appeared to be escaping to the west. The destroyer, still dodging for all she was worth, laid down smoke and made off in the direction of Malta at her best speed.

"Good luck and Godspeed," murmured Tyrwhitt to the fleeing destroyer.

The remaining French ships were now burning wrecks. Allied destroyers came in close to fish survivors out of the water and administer the *coup de grace* by sinking the flaming hulks with torpedoes.

The entire battle had taken less than an hour. Now the victors completed their task, as the big guns quickly reduced the port facilities of Tunis to rubble and ashes. King-Hall hoped that everyone had had time to leave the area before the bombardment.

Dinner that night in the officer's mess was quieter than usual. King-Hall was lost in his thoughts and did not say a word during the meal. After the meal, over brandy, Commodore Tyrwhitt said, "This was your first experience observing combat, Mr. King-Hall. Do you care to share your thoughts with us?"

"Yes, sir, if you wish to hear them," replied the Sub-Lieutenant. "At first I was wondering what I would have done had I been in that French admiral's place today. Was anything gained that could justify the sacrifice of his men by what was, after all, nothing but suicide?"

"Perhaps it wasn't his decision," speculated the Executive Officer. "The French Admiralty may have been under pressure from Paris to end the string of surrenders, and show some fight, even if it was a hopeless situation. In which case, poor old... DePay, was it?... may have been under orders from Paris to sacrifice his force to show the public that France was still fighting, or some such thing."

"That did occur to me, after a while," King-Hall agreed. "I wonder if that was the true explanation. I suppose we'll never know." He fell silent for a moment, and then he went on.

"After that, I began thinking about what will happen down here in the Mediterranean after the war." He turned to Commodore Tyrwhitt. "Sir, no matter what happens, when the war ends this Sea is going to be under the control of the Triple Alliance. We'll still have our squadron in Alexandria and our base in Malta, but the Germans, Italians and Austrians together will have a much bigger force than any the Royal Navy can commit here. The French Navy will be out of the game; it practically is now. So if the Kaiser and his chums decide to push us out of the Mediterranean..."

"You left out the Turks," added Lieutenant-Commander Summers. "You will recall that they have two shiny new dreadnoughts we built for them and just delivered to Constantinople last month."

The Exec was referring to the *Reshadieh* and *Sultan Osman*, modern dreadnoughts built in Britain for the Ottoman Empire, with thirteen and a half inch main batteries, and top speeds of twenty-one knots. There had been some talk of requisitioning the two ships for the Royal Navy, back at the beginning of August, when it looked as if Britain might get into the war. But when the Germans did not invade Belgium as expected, His Majesty's Government had no reasonable excuse for withholding the two ships which had been paid for in part with the pennies of Turkish schoolchildren, from the Ottomans. Since the Turks were much more likely to be found at the side of Germany and her allies than with Great Britain in the near future, the Exec was suggesting that these two ships should also be included in King-Hall's calculations of the naval strength of Britain's future enemies.

"I agree with you Mr. Summers, that we should expect to see the Turks added into the scales against us," said the Commodore Tyrwhitt. "Mr. King-Hall, I am pleased when I see a young officer who takes the time to think about the larger world outside his immediate duties and the ship to which he is assigned. You are not the first to have pondered the dangers of the situation that you have so succinctly outlined for us. You will no doubt be pleased to learn that some our colleagues, whose vision extends further than what can be seen from the bridge of a warship, have already given thought to these very matters. My own view is that no alliance lasts forever, so that the present dominance of the German coalition in the Mediterranean is unlikely to become a permanent reality. Italy and Austria, yes and the Ottomans too, have all had their little and not so little disagreements in the past, and undoubtedly will again in the future. I do not expect the current alliance system to outlast the war by very many years. In any case, Mr. King-Hall, you may take my word for it when I tell you that, in the Admiralty and the Foreign Office, better minds than any of ours have been considering a post-war world in which the Teutonic powers are victorious. I daresay that they are pondering it at Number 10 Downing Street, as well. The dangers are not, perhaps, so very hard to imagine, but preparing for them, ah, that is more difficult. If this war goes on as it has begun, I fear that our nation and our Empire will be in grave danger at its end. We will need all our wisdom and all our courage in the perilous time that I believe will follow. Thank you, gentlemen, for an interesting evening."

This was King-Hall's signal. As the most junior officer on the ship, it was his duty to make the traditional toast at the end of the evening meal. He rose from the table and all the other officers came to their feet as well. "Gentlemen, to the King," he said, downing the remaining brandy in his glass. All the officers echoed, "To the King!" and emptied their glasses in honor of King George V.

That night, King-Hall had difficulty falling asleep for the first time since he had come aboard the

Southampton. He lay on his back in his bunk in the darkness, his fingers laced behind his head.

The entire situation was just *wrong*, he decided. The Royal Navy should be blockading the German ports, keeping the High Seas fleet cowering in Wilhelmshaven and Cuxhaven, carrying out its traditional duty for the Empire, not sitting at anchor in Scapa Flow while Germany and her friends blithely won control of the seas. King-Hall had been so impressed by the description of sea power by the great American naval historian, Alfred Thayer Mahan, that he had committed it to memory. It was "the possession of that overbearing power on the sea which drives the enemy's flag from it, or allows it to appear only as a fugitive by controlling the great common..."

At the price of hundreds of ships and thousands of men, in great battles from Nelson's victory at Trafalgar onward, the Royal Navy had won dominance of the oceans of the world, defeating every rival that had arisen to challenge it. Was all that sacrifice, courage and tradition to be thrown away so that Germany, a nation without the slightest naval tradition, could displace the greatest navy in history?

When you came down to it, the British Empire was not much more than an idea, and an odd idea at that: a collection of disparate lands around the globe containing a hundred or more races and cultures, speaking God only knew how many languages, ruled for the benefit of all by the monarch of small island in Northern Europe. Only two things gave that idea substance, one symbolic and one very real.

The King was the symbol, the living embodiment of the Empire, to whom all his varied peoples, white, black or yellow, looked. The substantial one was the sea power exercised by the Royal Navy, whose control of the world's oceans linked together far-flung territories from the Hudson Bay, Canada to Port Stanley in the Falklands, from Delhi, India to Kingston, Jamaica. The

Empire's very existence was dependent on the Royal Navy's unchallenged supremacy of the sea. The British Empire should be in this war, not to save France and Russia, but because to sit it out would to allow the German challenger to believe that the Royal Navy was no longer to be feared, and that Germany was a match for Great Britain on the sea, the young sub-Lieutenant thought. And *that* was more dangerous than the temporary weakness in the Mediterranean Sea they had debated over dinner. It might very well prove to be fatal to the British Empire.

General Helmut von Moltke enjoying a light moment

Kaiser Wilhelm pondering English perfidy

The Stadtschloss, Berlin

Sir Edward Grey has a headache

Ambassador Paul Cambon pondering English perfidy

Ray Swing is skeptical

A serious Lieutenant Joseph Stilwell

"We who are about to die…" *Poilus*, circa 1914

French fortifications near Alsace, 1914

The Neiman River, East Prussia

Germans crossing a
pontoon bridge on the Eastern Front, 1915

"Have a good time, boys!" The Kaiser's legions off to war.

Lt. Colonel Max Hoffman preparing something unpleasant for the Russians

German machine-gun nest, East Prussia

Russian infantrymen eager to get at the Hun, 1914

Lt. Commander Stephen King-Hall, 1915

Commodore Reginald Tyrwhitt wondering how he
would look in an Admiral's hat

Light Cruiser H.M.S. *Southampton*

French Armored Cruiser *Edgar Quinet*

Chapter Eight: East of Warsaw, October 19, 1914

The List Regiment, along with the rest of the 6th Bavarian Division, had been transferred from the Sixth Army in Alsace to a new assignment with Hausen's Third Army in Poland. After four days in transit, the 6th Company ended billeted in a village so tiny and impoverished that it did not seem to have a name. It consisted mainly of a few filthy, thatch-roofed log cabins straggling along either side of the main street - a dirt, or rather mud, road. There was also a larger, although equally ramshackle, two-story building that seemed to combine the functions of store, post office and city hall. This was taken over as the company Headquarters.

The only other habitable structures were stone barns behind three of the (comparatively) more substantial houses. The barns were quickly occupied by the German soldiers, as they were more solidly built than the houses and smelled better. The inhabitants had fled before the rumor of the approaching invaders, taking with them their miserable personal possessions, their skinny goats and their scrawny chickens, leaving the nameless village a ghost town by the time the 6th Company entered.

The Austrian private was neither surprised at the obvious squalor and poverty of the Polish settlement, nor dismayed at having to bivouac in such a dismal place. It was only to be expected that the Poles would live like pigs, he thought. It was in their natures. Where the other men griped about being quartered in the little stinkhole of a town, the Austrian saw nothing to complain about, except being forced to wait for another opportunity to meet the enemy in action.

The transfer of the 6th Division had been conducted in a frantic rush to get the unit in position in time to join the big offensive in the East. The scuttlebutt was that this offensive was going to round up most of the Russian Army north of the Carpathians in an immense battle of envelopment, and possibly knock Russia right out of the war. As might be expected in the mad scramble of the movement, equipment had been left behind, and the forgotten supplies discovered only after the division had finally settled in its new slot in the line southeast of the provincial capital of Russian Poland. The Regiment's entire stock of extra soles for their boots had failed to make the trip, along with all the rest of the cobbler's supplies, including all the waterproof boot polish, among other things. The worst blow was the disappearance of all of the replacement barrels for the 6th Company's machine guns. (The Maxim was an excellent weapon in many ways, but its weakness was the tendency of the barrels to overheat and warp if the gunners were obliged to fire continuously without giving the guns a chance to cool off, which often happened in combat.) Without the spare barrels, the company's machine guns would be out of action in short order, if there was any heavy fighting.

During the transfer, the men were crammed together like cattle on troop trains for three days, with a short break to change trains at the Russian border where the German standard gauge tracks ended and the Russian wide-gauge ones began. They were then marched over the muddy paths that passed for roads in Poland, slogging on through the night in the rain without stopping for sleep or food. They kept on their feet by cramming down dry bread and stale cheese, and washing these "meals" down with schnapps. The division arrived exhausted but on schedule, only to discover that the big show had been postponed until the weather cleared and the roads had a chance to dry. The rain, which had been bad enough in central Poland where the List Regiment was traveling, had been positively torrential in the north. The whole insane hurry, the ghastly train ride followed by the forced marches in the rain, had all been for nothing.

It drove the Austrian nearly mad when he heard his comrades complaining about trivial matters like leaky boots or lost uniforms. Even worse, they made disloyal comments about their superiors, calling them "paper-shuffling General Staff REMFs" and the like, and whined that incompetents in Berlin had put them through an idiotic pell-mell rush for no reason. Did they not understand the importance of the work in which they were all engaged, opening new, fertile land to the Aryan race, correcting the historical accident that had allowed the subhuman Poles and Slavs to occupy it?

Still less could he understand why the regimental officers blithely ignored all the defeatist grumbling, disloyal criticisms of superior officers up to the General Staff, and even scurrilous comments and jokes... *jokes!*... about the Kaiser himself.

Although he knew that it would accomplish nothing, the Austrian was so incensed he had asked his company commander why the officers were allowing the enlisted men to commit what he saw as nothing short of treason. As usual, the Captain had not taken him seriously.

"They're not committing treason, Private," Captain Schmidt told him in a soothingly, as though he was talking to a peevish child. "They're just blowing off a little steam. What you are hearing is just the traditional griping of the foot soldier, which probably has been much the same since Roman times. I have no doubt that Julius Caesar's men complained much the same way, when they were routed out of their comfortable camps and marched off in the rain to chase wild Gauls through the forests. Such idle chatter is quite normal among combat soldiers," the Captain continued. "I can promise you it is not defeatist, and that none of this talk has any effect on morale or fighting spirit of the company or the Regiment. These are your comrades, brave soldiers, good men and loyal Germans, one and all." The Captain tactfully refrained from reminding the Austrian that he technically was not a German at all, having been born in Hapsburg Empire. "They are as good, brave and loyal as you. I'll take good care to monitor the company's morale, Private and all you'll have to worry about is killing Ivan. So what do you say we just forget about this whole business, and get on with the war?" he concluded, looking at the Austrian encouragingly.

The Austrian was disappointed by the Company Commander's reaction, but not surprised. Based on his thus far brief military experience, he had expected some such answer to his complaint. Very few of the officers or men in the Regiment had any idea of the real meaning of the work they were doing here in the East. To them, fighting the dregs of humanity like the Slavic racial trash they were facing was no different than fighting the comparatively pure French race.

Of course, the Austrian had tried to educate his comrades, to explain the historical significance of their mission. Whenever there was time and a handful of the men were gathered together, he would attempt to educate them about their duty to the Fatherland, and remind them of how fortunate they were to live in a time when they could participate in the fulfillment of Germany's historic destiny. He tried to share with them his vision of a future in which the Aryan race reigned supreme over the world. He explained the danger of allowing their pure blood to be diluted by mixing it with that of inferior peoples, or even worse, allowing it to be poisoned by the unspeakable Jew. On those rare occasions when he was not interrupted, he would then go on to describe the nature and purpose of the international Jewish-Marxist conspiracy, and how it must be defeated.

Usually, he was not able to get so far before he was shouted down. It hurt the Austrian when his comrades called him all sorts of names ranging from the relatively mild ones like "oddball" or "weirdo" to more the

97

pejorative "nut case" and "pain in the ass". Too many good German workingmen had been exposed to the Socialist virus at home and were now infected. To the Austrian, it was only further proof (not that any was needed) of how far the effects of the twin Jewish poisons of Marxism and Liberalism had spread, even into the ranks of the Army!

They could not appreciate how fortunate they were to be born in the only true German Empire, where the Aryan race was in the overwhelming majority, and had been able to keep itself reasonably pure. He had been unlucky enough to be born in the mongrel Austro-Hungarian Dual Monarchy, which had degenerated into a racial cesspool which grew more corrupt and vile with each passing year. He would have far rather gone to prison than fight to defend his decadent homeland. *That* was why he had dodged the draft when he was called up by the Austrian army, not because he was afraid. It was also why he had slipped across the border into Bavaria and, when the war broke out, and petitioned King Ludwig III for permission to volunteer for service in the Bavarian Army.

The Austrian was confident that by now no one in the entire List Regiment doubted his courage. He had *earned* his Iron Cross Second Class in combat, fearlessly exposing himself to heavy French fire while dragging his wounded platoon commander to safety. His comrades in the 6th Company might close their minds to his ideas, but there was not one of them who was unhappy to see the Austrian by his side in combat. Under the circumstances, he could hardly contain his joy when, after a week in the nameless Polish village, word came down that the roads were dry enough to launch the big offensive.

The Austrian crouched with the rest of the company in the shallow trench they had scraped out of the muddy soil, waiting for the preparatory bombardment to finish. He was impressed: this was the heaviest barrage he had seen yet. The Russian trenches were obscured by heavy smoke punctuated by gouts of flame and fountains of dirt from the shell bursts. Even from a kilometer away the waiting German soldiers could feel the earth shake under the pounding.

When the hurricane of shelling finally ended, the 6th Company, along with the rest of the List Regiment, and the entire Third Army rose as one and moved forward, not like an army of mere men, but like an irresistible force of nature, like a gray tide, into the East. The Austrian was a little surprised to hear the crackle of gunfire coming from the Russian lines. He had more than half-expected that the incredible artillery pounding would have killed any Russian foolish enough not to run away. For an instant, he wondered how such corrupted specimens of humanity could possess the courage to remain in position under such a bombardment to face the oncoming infantry assault, then concluded that, like beasts, they were simply too stupid to know when they were beaten.

As he moved forward, the Austrian heard bullets whine past on either side and overhead. The man on his right cried out and dropped face-first on the ground next to him. Ahead, he now could clearly hear the unmistakable rattle of a machine gun.

The Austrian acted almost without thinking. He threw himself into a crater from a shell that had landed short, an instant before a stream of bullets from the Russian Maxim gun sizzled over his hiding place. Slowly and cautiously, he raised his head to peer over the edge of the shell hole.

The Russian machine gun was protected by a sandbag revetment. It was being served by a crew of three brown-clad gunners, with another man pointing out targets. He waited until the crew's attention was focused in another direction and then slipped out of the hole and crawled rapidly on hands and knees through the mud, until he was only a few meters from the machine gun nest, but out of the view of the Russians. He lay flat on his back as another burst aimed at someone in the distance passed a few feet over his body. He pulled two small, round *kugel* hand grenades from his belt and laid them on the ground at his side. Then, taking one of the little metal spheres in his left hand, he pulled the wire that activated the black power igniter with his right. He held the now-live grenade for three long seconds, and then spun his body on the ground as he hurled it into the machine gun nest in a single motion. Without waiting for the explosion, the Austrian frantically ignited the other grenade and quickly threw it to join the first. The first grenade exploded in the middle of the gun crew while the second was still in the air. When he heard the second grenade detonate, he rolled to his feet, his rifle pointing forward, and charged the machine gun nest.

As it turned out, he had no need for the rifle. The two *kugels* had killed or incapacitated all four Russians. The Maxim gun had been knocked off its tripod base, and was now lying on the ground, the barrel bent in a "v". The Austrian suddenly felt dizzy, cold and sick. The muscles in his legs turned to water. He sank down shakily on a sandbag in the midst of the Russian corpses. The adrenaline that had driven his body to react at unnatural speed was gone, and he felt empty and weak.

In another moment he was surrounded by his mates. They cheered him, pounded his back and told him what a demon fighter he was. He was surprised to discover that he had been wounded in the leg at some point, although he had felt nothing at the time. The wound was in the meat of his thigh and was very bloody. Only after he saw the blood soaking through the leg of his trousers did the injury begin to throb. One of his comrades cut away the bloody cloth and bandaged him up.

He felt confused, disoriented. He tried to stand up, to re-join his comrades in the battle, but a hand gently pushed him back onto the stretcher on which he lay (when did they put him on a stretcher? he wondered foggily).

"Relax, Private," a voice said. "You've done enough fighting for one day." The Austrian looked up to see Captain Schmidt standing over him. "Half of the company saw you take out that machine gun nest. It was the bravest thing I ever saw. I am personally going to recommend you for an Iron Cross, First Class."

The Austrian's eyes widened in astonishment at this promise. The Iron Cross, First Class, was normally reserved for officers and NCOs. He had never heard of it ever being awarded to a private. Perhaps he had not heard the Captain correctly...

Captain Schmidt was smiling down at him, and nodding his head. "That's right, Private. I said the Iron Cross *First Class.* We will have to see about a promotion for you as well. I must go on with the company now, but I will see you again soon." The Captain patted the Austrian's good leg and ordered the stretcher bearers to take him back to the battalion aid station.

By the time he was released from the hospital to rejoin his unit, two weeks had gone by, the big offensive was over and the front had advanced thirty kilometers east of Warsaw. The offensive had been a success, he learned, dealing a heavy blow to the Russians, driving them back more than a hundred kilometers north and south of Warsaw, and capturing the capital of Russian Poland.

The Iron Cross ceremony was impressive. The entire Regiment was drawn up to see the Austrian and two other men awarded decorations for bravery. Colonel List himself pinned the medals on the recipients. The Austrian had not quite believed that he was really going to receive the Iron Cross First Class right up to the moment when the Colonel attached it to his chest.

Afterwards, his mates were not any more in agreement with the Austrian's political and racial views, but they were much more polite about their disagreement. This gave him almost as much satisfaction as the medal had.

The Captain had not forgotten about the promised promotion. The next time the 6th Company went into combat, they would do so with a freshly-minted lance corporal. The Austrian's heart swelled with pride when he reflected on the honors his homeland of choice had so generously heaped upon him, in spite of his foreign birth.

The Austrian had always believed he was destined for greatness. Now he knew for a certainty that his destiny and that of Germany were intertwined. That night, lying on his bed of heaped straw, he decided that it would be his fate to do something so important in the history of his adopted Fatherland, that if all the heroes of German history could somehow be resurrected and brought out of the past, from Arminius, Aryan conqueror of the Roman legions, to Frederick the Great, founder of the modern Prussian nation, to Bismarck creator of the newest and greatest triumph of Aryan genius, the Second Reich, a place would be found among them for a man born in Upper Austria in the little town of Braunau am Inn, a man named Adolf Hitler.

Chapter Nine: Washington D.C., October 29, 1914

William Jennings Bryan tilted his chair back and swiveled to look out the huge window of his office at the dome of the Capitol glittering in the afternoon sun.

He had long ago given up any hope of being elected President, and was now beginning to think that if that job was any more aggravating than his present position as Secretary of State, it was probably just as well he had never won the office. It was not the work he found trying, but rather the many demands for favors that crossed his desk. He was certain that the White House was flooded with ten times as many such requests.

Reluctant to return to the pile of unread papers on his desk, he opened the top drawer, and pulled out a souvenir from his 1896 Presidential campaign, a newspaper editorial that he had mounted in a picture frame to preserve it.

The editorial was from the *New York Herald*, a staunch Republican paper, announcing that the *Herald* was sponsoring a new candidate for President, a chimpanzee from the Bronx Zoo named William Grinning Organmonk. The *Herald* editorial writer took the position that "if the currency of the country is to be monkeyed with, our candidate is the one best qualified to do it."

This risible attack on Bryan's Free Silver platform never failed to bring a smile to his face. Was bi-metallism really such a terrible idea? he wondered. He still was not convinced it was, even after all these years and three defeats at the polls.

He shook his head, as if to clear away old memories, sighed, and turned back to the pile of papers stacked in his "In" box.

The first item was a letter from a Mr. Alba B. Johnson, President of the Baldwin Locomotive Works in

Philadelphia. This particular headache had been thoughtfully forwarded to State from the Navy Department under the endorsement of Assistant Secretary of the Navy Franklin Roosevelt. Bryan made a mental note to return the favor to Mr. Roosevelt sometime.

Mr. Johnson's letter stated that a French railroad known as the PLM had ordered two modified Class T-31 locomotives, custom-built for operations in the mountains, from his company in 1913 for delivery in 1914. Baldwin Locomotive Works had completed the machines in all particulars and a timely manner as specified by the contract, and had shipped them to the French port of Le Havre for delivery to PLM, as requested by the buyer.

Or rather, they had *attempted* to ship them to the buyer, by having them loaded aboard the freighter *St. Louis* in Philadelphia bound for Le Havre. However, before the ship and its cargo had been able to reach its destination, it had been stopped by a German destroyer in the North Sea. The captain of the German vessel (who Johnson characterized, rather harshly, Bryan thought, as "no better than a pirate") informed the skipper of the *St. Louis* that the port of Le Havre, and indeed all French ports, were now officially closed by blockade on order of His Imperial Majesty, Kaiser Wilhelm II, and that they were going to remain closed to all shipping for the duration of the war. In any event, the port facilities at Le Havre were unusable at the present time, having recently been reduced to rubble after a bombardment by a squadron of battlecruisers of the Imperial German High Seas Fleet. The German destroyer captain went on to suggest that the *St. Louis* would do well to return with its cargo from whence it came by the shortest, fastest route available, before both ship and cargo were seized as contraband of war and put into service hauling freight for the German Empire.

The captain of the freighter agreed that return was the wisest option, and so delivered the two custom-built T-31 locomotives back to the storage shed at the dock on the Delaware River in Philadelphia, where they now sat, running up Baldwin Locomotive's storage fees by the day.

Johnson concluded his letter with a demand that the government of the United States do something to put a stop to this unwarranted interference with legitimate business. He did not say exactly what the government should do, just that it should do *something,* and do that something without delay, as the Baldwin Locomotive Works and its stockholders were continuing to lose money due to the German Empire's illegal and outrageous interference. Since the letter had originally been addressed to the Navy Department, Bryan supposed that Johnson expected his locomotives to return to Europe escorted by a battleship, or possibly by the entire U.S. fleet, so that he could deliver his machines without any further difficulties.

It seemed to the Secretary of State that Mr. Alba Johnson was something like a locomotive himself; at least, he appeared to have a one-track mind. In addition, Johnson apparently had the ability to roll right over or through any facts that he did not wish to recognize, such as the war in Europe. It was possible that he *still* did not suspect that the problems he had encountered in attempting to deliver his machines to France might persist for as long as the war continued. Bryan wondered if a mere letter from the State Department would be enough to permit the concept to penetrate through to Mr. Johnson. In any case, the man was almost certainly a dyed-in-the-wool Republican, like most of the big capitalists, and Bryan saw no urgency in formulating an answer to his letter.

He sighed again, and put the letter aside for later, picking up in its place the weekly summary of the cause of Mr. Johnson's unhappiness, provided to him courtesy

105

of the War Department. Bryan shook his head as he read. He was a man of peace, and could not fathom what was driving the Europeans to cut each other's throats with such enthusiasm.

It seemed that the deadlock on the Western Front remained unchanged. The French government had finally admitted that their early offensives in Alsace had been thrown back, although they still claimed that they had inflicted greater casualties on the Germans than vice-versa. The War Department report was skeptical of this claim, and estimated that as a result of the heavy losses it had sustained in the fighting in Alsace, the French Army would be incapable of mounting any significant offensive operations until the spring of 1915 at the earliest.

In addition to the bad news from the front, the French economy was doing poorly, suffering from the effects of the German blockade. With the main French fleet still bottled up in Toulon by a powerful squadron of German ships, the French were helpless to stop the shelling of both their Atlantic and Mediterranean ports by the Germans, or to do anything at all about the complete disruption of maritime imports and exports. For France, the loss of the Baldwin locomotives represented one small drop in a sea of troubles.

Even with all these difficulties, France was doing well compared to its ally in the East. After the calamitous fighting in East Prussia where the Germans had destroyed two Russian field armies at the very outset of the war, the gray mass had rolled rapidly into Russian Poland and Lithuania, delayed more by the need to alter the Russian wide-gauge railways to German standards than by any great resistance put up by the Russians. Grand Duke Nicholas, commander of the Russian armies, had rushed his Fourth and Fifth Armies north from the Carpathians to stem the German tide, largely abandoning the successes gained in opening offensives against the Austrians in Galicia. Bryan consulted a map of Eastern Europe, putting his finger on the places named, then nodded and returned to the War Department summary.

The Grand Duke had attempted to hold the line of the Vistula River, with the defense centered on Warsaw. The German Second Army had forced a crossing of the Vistula north of Warsaw at the town of New Georglewisk, at the junction of the Vistula and Bug Rivers, (here Bryan consulted the map again), then turned south, nearly trapping the Russian Fourth Army in Warsaw.

The Russians had been forced into a headlong flight east to avoid encirclement. Desperate defensive efforts of the Russian Army combined with torrential rains had finally stopped the German advance. Still, the War Department estimated that along with Warsaw and a considerable slice of central Poland, the Russians had lost as many as 100,000 additional men and great quantities of equipment which they were obliged to abandon in the rush to get out of the German pincers.

The Germans had also rolled east along the Baltic coast at the same time they were flanking the Russians out of Warsaw. Forward elements of the German First Army had reached the shores of the Gulf of Riga in Latvia three days earlier, on the 26th, before being forced to stop by having outrun their supply train. The author of the War Department memorandum noted that the Germans were being greeted as liberators by huge crowds of local residents in Lithuania and Latvia. It appeared that the ethnic Latvian and Lithuanian majorities of the Baltic States had not been very happy under Russian rule.

The memorandum opined that the Russian losses, especially in artillery, but also in railway equipment, ammunition and even small arms could not easily be made good. Russia was cut off from any outside aid by the German Baltic Fleet in the north, and in the south by the Turkish fleet with its new dreadnoughts, which outclassed anything in the Russian Black Sea squadron. Moreover, the Russian economy was utterly dependent for foreign credits on the export of wheat, and the export trade was, because of the aforementioned blockade, currently non-existent. Therefore, even if the Russians could find a way to bring substantial quantities of munitions into the country (from the Pacific on the Trans-Siberian Railroad, or through Archangel on the Arctic Sea?), they had neither the hard currency nor any source of foreign credit to pay for them.

In case these troubles were not enough, there was more. The Russian Army was perpetually short of food, ammunition, transport and other essentials of modern war, of everything but men, in fact, because the government of the Czar was notoriously incompetent, inefficient and corrupt. Finally, there were well-founded reports that the ruling classes of Russian society and the Czar's ministries were riddled with defeatists, spies and German sympathizers.

"Outside of the occurrence of some unforeseen event," the memorandum concluded, "the short term prospects for Russia in the present war are poor, and do not appear likely to improve within the next twelve months."

Bryan replaced the War Department memorandum on his desk, shoved his chair backward, and, accompanied by the music of gently creaking springs, began to rock slowly back and forth, his fingers laced across his paunch and his eyes resting thoughtfully on the ceiling.

The Russian Empire was clearly in a bad way. The question was whether Czar Nicholas could see the hopelessness of his country's position as clearly as an outsider like Bryan could. Was it too early to consider offering to mediate a peace settlement? Bryan did not want to take the slightest risk of involving the United States in this insane war, but it would be a great act of Christian fellowship if he could somehow contribute to bringing the senseless slaughter to an end, and by so doing, he thought with a wry smile, do something to ease the troubled mind of Mr. Alba B. Johnson of the Baldwin Locomotive Works.

It was not too early to start thinking about it at any rate, he decided. Perhaps he should prepare a little note for Professor Wilson ("Professor" was his private nickname for the President) in the Oval Office, laying out some arguments for the U.S. to offer its good offices as an impartial arbiter for the warring parties. He scooted his chair back to the desk, removed a fountain pen from its holder, and began to write.

*

President Wilson sat in his chair, his back straight, his fingers steepled, peering at his Secretary of State through his pince-nez spectacles. As usual, the President's austere features were unreadable; Bryan could not tell whether the Professor approved, disapproved or was utterly indifferent to his idea.

"Aside from any moral considerations," Bryan continued, "it has wonderful political potential. Look how much favorable press Roosevelt got negotiating an end to the war in Siberia in 1905, and how much more when they gave him the Peace Prize," Bryan said, reminding Wilson that Theodore Roosevelt had mediated the Treaty of Portsmouth that had ended the Russo-Japanese War back in 1905 and been awarded the Nobel Prize for it.

"It's not too early to start thinking about the 1916 election. There is probably not going to be a significant third party to split their votes this time, and the Republicans are still biggest party in the country," he continued.

Bryan, a little tactlessly perhaps, was reminding Wilson that he was a minority president, who owed his victory in the 1912 to a split in the Republican Party, when Roosevelt had run as a Progressive against the incumbent Taft. The two Republicans had together totaled 50 percent of the vote, while Wilson had received only 42 percent (the Socialist candidate, Eugene Debs had taken most of the remainder).

Wilson pondered this for a moment, and then nodded judiciously. "I cannot at the moment see any grave hazard in proposing the services of this nation as an impartial arbiter, to bring about an equitable termination of the present conflict." As usual, the pompous Professor used three words where one would do, and long ones at that. Bryan had difficulty keeping his eyes from rolling up towards the Oval Office ceiling.

"Our ability to bring about a pacific resolution of the current hostilities is dependent, however, on the inclination of the contending coalitions to negotiate," he continued. "Is there any evidence to indicate that they are?"

"Not yet, maybe," Bryan conceded. "But the way the war is going in the east, the Czar will probably have to sue for peace within the next twelve months, or even sooner. If that happens, the French will be on their own. How long will they be able to stay in the war alone against Germany, Italy, and Austria while still under the German blockade? I imagine that Monsieur Vivani, or whoever is in power in Paris by then, will be looking for any way out short of total surrender. If we offer to arbitrate now, I agree that neither side will be ready. But, when the time comes…"

"The seed that has been sown will have had an opportunity to germinate," Wilson finished for him. "Yes, it is worthwhile to make the endeavor. The benefits of peace will go not merely to the nations now engaged in the present conflict, but to all the peoples of the world, through the resumption of the normal flow of international commerce."

Bryan was again reminded of the difficulties the war was causing for Alba Johnson and the Baldwin Locomotive Works. The thought passed quickly as Wilson's lecture continued.

"We can hope that someday all disputes between sovereign nations will be settled without recourse to violent confrontation, but instead by referral to a neutral adjudicator for arbitration, and wars between nations will looked upon as part of a savage, primeval stage in the social evolution of mankind, long since outgrown," the President pontificated. "If we are fortunate enough to be permitted to bring this European conflict to an end, that perhaps will be the first step on the road to a future in which mankind is spared the horrors of war."

Bryan thought Wilson a bit premature to talk about eradicating war itself, especially since the American proposal had not even been made to the parties yet. He also slightly resented the way the Professor now sounded as if he had thought of the whole thing himself. But, despite that, despite the self-important way he had made this little speech, Bryan could not help but agree in his heart with the sentiments the President had expressed.

"May a merciful God grant us such a gift," he said. The Secretary of State closed his eyes and bowed his head in silent prayer. After a brief moment of hesitation, he was joined by the President.

Chapter Ten: Berlin, January 25, 1915

Ray Swing was lucky to find an empty table in the Guildhall Rathskeller beneath the Municipal Tower that housed the offices of the Berlin city government. It was only because he had come in an off hour, at 2:30 in the afternoon that he had been able to get a table at all. The circular dining hall was immense, able to accommodate more than 1000 customers at one sitting. Even so, during the busiest times, at midday or between 5 and 6 in the evening, the establishment was so full that customers would stand behind the chairs of those fortunate enough to obtain a seat, waiting for them to finish so that they could sit in turn.

At such times, the Rathskeller was a madhouse, filled with shouting, smoking, eating and especially drinking Berliners. Swing could not understand how anyone could stand it, but the Germans seemed to love the atmosphere of the place. The combination of cacophonous din and thick clouds of malodorous cigar fumes invariably gave the American a headache.

Well, *he* hadn't picked the Rathskeller for his meeting with Stilwell. As the big, outdoor beer gardens were closed during the cold Northern European winter, the American spymaster and military attaché was forced to select an indoor location, and this was it.

Before a waiter could take his order, Swing was joined by Stilwell. The latter was, as was usual on such occasions, wearing civilian clothing. He was dressed much like Swing himself, with a long, brown woolen topcoat over a dark suit.

Stilwell settled into a chair and remarked, "The Krauts do like their beer, don't they?" He indicated a rather garish fresco on the huge column in the center of the enormous circular dining room. It depicted a pair of rollicking male university students in the company of a pretty young girl drawing beer from a keg. Underneath

112

the painting was inscribed a poem which Stilwell recited aloud:

"When beauty's eyes are smiling near,
And loving hands present the beer,
Then in a glorious dream we rise,
Into the realms of Paradise!"

"Brings tears to your eyes, doesn't it?" he asked sardonically.

Swing, whose taste in poetry ran towards Edgar Allen Poe, replied, "Yeah, Joe, it's just lovely. What's worth ordering here, besides beer, that is?"

Stilwell studied the menu. "The food here is OK, but I wouldn't risk getting anything too elaborate. I would stick with the *rindfliesch* with *kartofflen*, if I were you."

A moment later, an apron-clad waiter with a waxed and fully outspread Kaiser Wilhelm mustache came bustling up to the table to take their orders. Stilwell ordered a beer, but no food. Swing, who had not eaten all day, ordered a plate of beef and roast potatoes to accompany his lager.

After the waiter left them, Stilwell said quietly. "Thanks for the dope on the new *minenwerfer*." One of Swing's contacts in the German Army's Experimental Weapons Section had provided details of a new 7.8 centimeter mine-thrower that had been developed for blasting through fieldworks in preparation for an infantry assault.

"Do you have anything on that other 'innovation' we discussed?" Stilwell asked. "The... uh..." he held his hand to his throat, and coughed lightly, preferring not to speak the words "poisonous gas" aloud.

Swing leaned forward, and said in a low tone, "They tried it, Joe. They used 18,000 shells of some stuff called methylbenzyl bromide at Bolimow, a town north of Warsaw, two weeks ago."

113

Stilwell nodded. "No point in making the stuff if you're not going to use it. So, what happened?"

Swing shook his head. "It was a flop. It didn't do a thing. The Russians apparently didn't even notice that anything unusual was going on. As it turns out, it doesn't work at low temperatures. I'll get the details to you at the drop tomorrow." They had worked out a system of passing on information by leaving notes folded in a newspaper on a particular park bench in the Tiergarten. Swing hated what he saw as dime-novel nonsense, but he was by now resigned to its necessity.

"Okay," Stilwell said. "Anything else?"

"Yes," Swing said. "They already have something a lot stronger in the works: bi-chloride gas. The bromine is supposed to incapacitate by irritating the eyes and throat, causing tearing and coughing. Chlorine eats away the eyes and destroys lung tissue: it kills. A big-shot chemist named Haber is working on it over at the Kaiser Wilhelm Institute. My guy in the War Ministry doesn't know exactly when they'll be ready to roll it out, but it will probably be sometime in the spring."

"That will be a nice treat for the Russkies, as if they didn't have enough trouble already," Stilwell commented. "Speaking of trouble, how are things out at the front? I'd like to go and see for myself, but between my official work for the Embassy, my unofficial work for DepWar and the way the Krauts worry I am going to get them bad press by getting myself killed, I don't get much of a chance."

"The front has been pretty static, other than local line-straightening attacks like the one at Bolimow, for a couple of reasons," Swing said. "First, given how lousy the roads are, winter is not exactly the ideal season for launching a major offensive in Poland. Second, there are still logistical problems. The Germans are still converting Russian wide-gauge track to standard gauge and rounding up more wide-gauge locomotives and rolling stock. They are going to keep having supply problems until they get the rail system in Poland organized. I don't expect anything big to break until spring. In fact, I'm staying on here for a few weeks to try to catch up on my office work."

"I'm hearing the same thing from my sources," Stilwell said. "The big Warsaw Offensive in the spring depleted the Krauts' stockpiles of practically everything. Rumor has it that they're building up again, with an eye towards a push all along the front in April, a big one, even bigger than the October offensive."

"I wonder if they'll have the new gas ready by then?" Swing asked.

"I don't know about that, but I will guarantee one thing: if they do have it, you can be sure that they'll want to see what it can do right away," Stilwell said. "Once again, Germany brings the benefits of modern science to the world," he finished sourly.

Swing nodded. "Better living through chemistry,", he said.

Chapter Eleven: Off Toulon, February 8, 1915

King-Hall was taken by surprise when, just after nine hundred hours, the ship's bells calling the crew to action stations announced that the French were coming out of Toulon for a fight.

The three light cruisers that comprised the 1st Light Cruiser Observation Squadron had been quietly watching Admiral Reinhard Scheer's High Seas Battle Fleet since November. They had been given this assignment after the Triple Alliance Mediterranean Squadron under Admiral Wilhelm Souchon that they had been following was disbanded.

Souchon's fleet had completed its assignment by demolishing the harbor facilities of the last of the French North African ports and seizing or sinking all the French Navy vessels and merchantmen they found. The Austrian ships returned to winter in their home port of Pola, the Italians to Taranto on the heel of the Italian boot, and the Germans to join the blockade of the French Atlantic coast, back home to Wilhelmshaven or sent to carry out various errands in the colonies.

From almost the first hour *Southampton* and her companions *Birmingham* and *Nottingham* entered Genoa to take on fuel before moving onto their station off the Rivera, rumors that the French were about to sortie from their base to challenge the Germans were everywhere. King-Hall had heard them; every officer and able seaman in the squadron had heard them. But after days, then weeks went by and nothing happened, he decided that the rumors were unfounded, and for a very good reason.

On its face, the idea of the French staging a stand-up slugging match with the German High Seas Fleet was nonsensical. The main French battle-fleet, designated

116

the 1st *Armeé Navale,* was based in Toulon and built around 4 dreadnought battleships, two of them so new they had not completed their sea trials when the war began. The dreadnoughts were of the 1911 *Courbet* class: *Paris*, *Jean Bart*, *France* and *Courbet*. They were said to be excellent ships of the most modern design, sporting 12 twelve-inch guns, protected by 10 1/2 inch armor belts and boasting top speeds in excess of 20 knots. They were justifiably the pride of the French Navy and probably the equals ship-for-ship of any vessels afloat.

The rest of the 1st *Armee Navale's* battle line was not as impressive. In addition to the four dreadnoughts, there were six older battleships of the *Danton* class. The *Dantons* were considered semi-dreadnoughts, turbine-powered like the newer types, but still mounting the typical mixed main armament characteristic of pre-1905 capital ships, with four 12-inch guns, and twelve 9.6 inch guns. They were slower, less well armed and had thinner armored belts than their younger sisters. They would not fare well in a slugging match with real dreadnoughts.

There were also nine pre-dreadnought battleships of various classes. The consensus among the officers on the *Southampton* was that these obsolete ships would be useful in action only to the extent that they drew enemy fire away from the other French ships.

The French Toulon fleet also had available for action sixteen armored cruisers of various types similar to the ones under the late Rear Admiral Emile DuPay that had been sent to the bottom of the sea off Tunis in September. Also available were several obsolete protected cruisers and a fairly large number of destroyers, of which perhaps fifty or so were in battle-worthy condition. Presiding over this not inconsiderable force was Admiral Augustin de Lapeyrère, a canny veteran who had been called out of retirement to take command in his country's darkest hour.

The German fleet that waited off the coast was so powerful that a French sortie against it would be an act of recklessness verging on madness. Admiral Scheer commanded a force of *sixteen*(!) dreadnought battleships, of the *Nassau*, *Helgoland*, *Kaiser* and *Konig* classes respectively, equipped with Krupp guns, varying from twelve 11.5 inch rifles on the oldest ships, the 1908 *Nassau*s, to ten 12-inchers on the newest, the 1913 *Konig* class.

All the German dreadnoughts had armor belts of at least 12 inches, and all were designed to be practically unsinkable, with extensive watertight compartmentation and double hulls running nearly the entire length of the ships. Each of them was as formidable as the French *Courbet*s, and there were four times as many of the Germans.

In the unlikely event that Scheer was worried that a fourfold superiority in modern battleships would not be sufficient, he was no doubt soothed by the presence of six of the newest type of capital ship, the battle-cruisers. These had been used to bombard the French Atlantic ports at the war's outset, and later did blockade duty in the North Sea until early in the new year. In January, they were replaced by destroyers and light cruisers, and sent to join the Scheer in the Mediterranean.

These ships were armed with 11 1/2 or 12-inch main batteries like the battleships, but were faster. The *Von der Tann*, for example, was designed to *cruise* at 24 knots, and was rumored to have a flank speed of nearly *30* knots, faster even than the far smaller and more lightly armed *Southampto*n. This astonishing speed was gained at the cost of protection. The *Von der Tann*'s main armor belt was only four inches thick over most of the hull, and the other five German battlecruisers had even less protection. They were designed to outrun and out-gun any armored cruiser in existence, and there was no doubt that they could. It was the development of this class of ship that had made the French armored cruisers, indeed the whole class of armored cruisers, virtually obsolete.

Scheer also had plenty of escorts for the big ships in the form of armored cruisers, light cruisers and swarms of destroyers. In sum, the German fleet off Toulon was present in overwhelming strength. In King-Hall's view, if Lapeyrère offered battle, there could only ensue another massacre like the Battle of Tunis, but on a far larger and bloodier scale.

That was why King-Hall tended to dismiss the rumors of a sortie. If he, a lowly sub-lieutenant, could see how forlorn the French hope for victory in a straight-up battle would be, certainly the experienced and intelligent Admiral Lapeyrère could see it as well. Every week that passed with no battle occurring simply went to confirm his conclusion that there was not going to be one.

But now it seemed that there would be a fight after all. When King-Hall arrived on the bridge panting, a little after racing up two ladders to the bridge, Commodore Tyrwhitt was already present with Lieutenant Commander Summers in command, on the bridge. (Captain Goodenough had come down with some kind of galloping awfuls in his bowels, and had been put ashore at Malta to recover.)

"Set course at one-three-zero, if you please, Mr. Summers. Engines at three-quarters full," the Commodore ordered, as calmly as if he was ordering toast with marmalade for breakfast. After the acting captain echoed these orders for the helmsman, Tyrwhitt said, "Kindly signal Captain Duff and Captain Miller..." (the skippers of the *Birmingham* and *Nottingham*, respectively) "...to conform their ships to our movements."

King-Hall realized that the Commodore was taking the squadron directly away from the impending battle. Something of his dismay must have shown on his face when Tyrwhitt turned and saw him on the bridge.

"Never fear, Mr. King-Hall," he said. "We aren't going very far from the action. But I should like to reduce as much as possible the likelihood of having one of our ships being hit by a stray 12-inch shell. My orders from the Admiralty are very clear on that point: they do not want any of our ships sunk by either French or German fire. It might cause a diplomatic incident."

The other bridge officers laughed nervously at this remark, and the Commodore allowed himself a thin smile. "The squadron will cruise to 15 miles south-east of Cape Cepet, and then take up positions from which we may observe the coming battle. I do not expect it to last more than a few hours."

It was difficult to make sense out of what was happening back to the northeast, where the fighting was going on. King-Hall had been able to see through his high-powered field glasses the opening phase of the battle clearly enough, as the rival destroyer and cruiser squadrons clashed, each attempting to press home torpedo attacks on the opponent's big ships. He saw the German main battle line form up and steam in the direction of the more distant French fleet. Thereafter, although the orange muzzle flashes of the battleships' main batteries, the fountaining water of misses and the violent explosions of the hits were plain to see, it was impossible to get a real picture of how this, the first naval battle in history to pit dreadnought against dreadnought, was progressing.

King-Hall saw something, a big ship, a battleship of some kind probably, take a direct hit and explode violently, sending a pillar of flame hundreds of feet into the pale blue sky, followed by a mushrooming cloud of black smoke. The ship split in two pieces and vanished beneath the waves in less than a minute. There was no way to identify the unlucky ship, or even to be sure to which navy it had belonged.

"Direct hit on the main powder magazine, I should think," commented Lieutenant Commander Summers, who had come out on the wing of the bridge, and was observing the battle alongside King-Hall. "Wouldn't be surprised if the entire crew went to the bottom with her."

King-Hall shivered to think that the lives of the entire crew of the unfortunate ship, perhaps as many as a thousand men, had just disappeared in the blink of an eye. He was sharply reminded that he was not a spectator at a tennis match; the game being played out before him was in deadly earnest.

By thirteen hundred hours, the distant booms of the guns were becoming less frequent. They ceased altogether by fourteen-thirty, and the ships remaining that were not burning wrecks all flew flags bearing the black cross on white ground with an eagle at the center, a black cross over red, white and black stripes in the upper left quadrant, the battle ensign of the Imperial German Navy. German cruisers and destroyers moved among the wrecks, picking up survivors and finishing off the floating hulks with torpedoes. The remaining French vessels had evidently withdrawn back to port behind the minefields that guarded the approaches to Toulon.

At fifteen hundred hours, Commodore Tyrwhitt sent a wireless message to Admiral Scheer requesting permission for the British cruisers to approach and aid in the rescue work. The request was promptly granted, and the three Royal Navy ships quickly went into action. Aided by searchlights, the rescue effort continued well into the night. By the time Commodore Tyrwhitt finally called off the search at 0:30 hours, the British cruisers had fished more than a hundred French sailors from the sea.

By the third day after the battle, which was being called the Battle of Cape Cepet in the German dispatches, it was clear that the French Navy had suffered a major defeat. The French sailors pulled out of the water by the Observation Squadron were questioned to discover the names of their ships and what they personally witnessed of the battle. When this information was combined with reports from observers from all three Royal Navy cruisers, Commodore Tyrwhitt was able to prepare what he felt was a reasonably accurate picture of the French losses in the action in his report to the Admiralty in London. One thing they had determined was that the French battleship that had blown up so spectacularly was the semi-dreadnought *Danton*, which had apparently taken practically her entire crew of 681 officers and men to the bottom with her.

They also found a few German sailors Scheer's ships had overlooked. At least one German capital ship had been lost, the *Posen*, one of the 1907 *Nassau* class, the oldest German dreadnought types. Evidently she had either been torpedoed by a French submarine or had struck a mine. In any case, the ship had been holed below the waterline and had sunk quickly with heavy loss of life.

King-Hall's private forebodings about the future of the British Empire were renewed. Without a fleet, how was France to defend her colonial possessions in the Far East and in the Western Hemisphere? And if she could not defend them, would they then fall into the hands of the German Empire? *There* was a nightmare to be reckoned with: a powerful German fleet with bases all over the world, able to endanger every part of the British Empire, a more dangerous rival than any it had faced since Napoleon.

Chapter Twelve: Hanoi, February 17, 1915

Joost van Vollenhoven stared out the window of his office in the Governor General's Palace. Framed in the big window looking down on the street was a column of brown-clad Japanese infantry marching along the palm-lined boulevard below. Although he appeared to be looking at the soldiers, Vollenhoven in fact saw nothing. He was preoccupied with trying to recall the architectural details of his official residence and the center of French administration of the colony of Indochina. This was the Italian Renaissance style Governor's Palace, the very building in which he now stood.

Every element of the building, from the broken pediments with their Ionic pilasters in the façade, to the grand staircase sweeping up to the formal *piano nobile* for official receptions, to the little Roman shrines over the elaborate doorways (he had been told that they were called "aedicules"), was there to make a statement. The statement was roughly: "As this building was built by white men, so this colony is ruled by white men, and so it shall ever be, for the white race is naturally superior and born to rule over the yellow, brown and black races. You, fortunate subjects of the Republic of France, Khmer from the south, Bahner from the central highlands, Katu from Laos, whatever the name of your backward tribe or primitive culture, all will be granted the gifts of French civilization and culture: white schools, white roads and trains, white medicine, white literature, philosophy and art, so that someday you may reach the highest level of achievement possible for the yellow races by becoming second-rate white men."

This pretty well summed up the attitude of the French Colonial Administration for as long as he had been associated with it. Vollenhoven was proud of his adopted country (he had born in Rotterdam), and he had never for a single day regretted the fifteen years he had spent in her colonial service, but he found the (alleged) thought processes of most Colonial Office civil servants to be idiotically bigoted, incredibly hidebound and remarkably chauvinistic. They shared a peculiar ability to reject any facts that failed to fit into their world picture. Here in Indochina, for example, he had subordinates who had managed to spend years in the colony without ever learning that civilization in Southeast Asia dated back to 2800 B.C., when their own ancestors were primitive, skin-clad wanderers in the gloomy forests of Northern Europe.

When he was 22, Vollenhoven had taken French citizenship, and entered the *Ecole Coloniale* to train for a career in colonial administration. He had been a starry-eyed idealist back then, who truly believed that the advanced European nations had a duty to those parts of the world that were less fortunate than they.

"Take up the White Man's burden-
Send forth the best ye breed-
Go bind your sons to exile
To serve your captives' need;
To wait in heavy harness,
On fluttered folk and wild-
Your new-caught, sullen peoples,
Half-devil and half-child.

"Take up the White Man's burden-
The savage wars of peace-
Fill full the mouth of Famine
And bid the sickness cease;
And when your goal is nearest
The end for others sought,
Watch sloth and heathen Folly
Bring all your hopes to naught."

124

He had read Kipling's famous poem just after he received his law degree, and was still wondering what to do with his life. The exhortation in the verses struck a chord in Vollenhoven; he *did* want to help bring an end to famine and epidemic, to break the age-old cycle of poverty and misery that trapped these unfortunate peoples. After he had finished a stint in the Army (a useful experience for anyone who wished to rise in the Colonial Service), he took a position with the Colonial Ministry bureaucracy in Paris, his goal always to obtain an appointment overseas, to work with and for the people who had come involuntarily under the rule of France. It was not until 1905 that the opportunity came: a posting as Secretary-General to the Governor of French Equatorial Africa. He was still a bureaucrat perhaps, but at least he was working in the colonies. In 1907, he was made acting Governor of two French West African colonies, first Senegal, and then Guinea.

In his African posts he had tried to give the natives some measure of self-government, acting as much as possible through local tribal leaders chosen by the people themselves. He had also tried to soften the harshest effects of economic exploitation by the mother country.

Then, just a little more than a year ago, he had been appointed Governor-General of Indochina. The colony had a long history of unrest and dissatisfaction with French rule. The most recent sign of it had been in the late 1880's, when the *Can Vuong* rebellion broke out. It was only put down after four years of fighting and heavy loss of life. Ever since, although there had been no major outbreaks, under a surface calm the colony seethed with nationalist and revolutionary ferment. Reports from lower level colonial agents and unofficial native sources led him to expect another revolutionary outbreak in the very near future. Vollenhoven had hoped to discover the roots causes of the unrest and act to ameliorate them before another wave of violence began, but in the short time he had been in the office he had only begun to understand the basic problems and as yet had no solutions to offer.

Now it seemed that he would not have the responsibility of dealing with the nationalist uprising that he was certain would explode within the next year or two. That would fall to Indochina's new proprietors, who would soon discover that they had stolen a hornet's nest. It was no less than they deserved.

He was brought back from his musings to the present by the almost apologetic sound of his visitor clearing his throat. Here in the office of the Governor General of Indochina was a representative of one of the yellow races who emphatically did *not* accept the idea of white superiority.

Vollenhoven turned away from the window to look at the bespectacled little Oriental man in a cream suit standing on the other side of his desk, dabbing at beads of sweat on his forehead with a white handkerchief.

"I'm terribly sorry about turning you out of your residence, but it should only be for a short time, Your Excellency," said Mr. Irakawa, the newly appointed Administrator for the Imperial Japanese Protectorate of Indochina. "As you know, the Protectorate is only a temporary measure, and I can assure you that once the present crisis has ended…"

"The temporary Protectorate of Indochina will be dissolved, to be immediately replaced by the Imperial Japanese Colony of Indochina," the Governor-General interrupted. "I am not a potted plant, Mr. Irakawa. You might give me a little credit for being able to see what your government is doing, especially since it is making almost no effort to clothe its naked aggression with even the tiniest fig-leaf of legality."

A pained expression spread over the face of the Japanese bureaucrat. "Please, Mr. Governor-General, I understand your strong feelings under the circumstances,

126

but I beg you not to make the situation out to be worse than it actually is. There is no cause to employ intemperate language like 'naked aggression', or to make hasty, unwarranted assumptions regarding the future of the colony," he protested. "The Emperor is reluctantly taking this step to safeguard the interests of both ourselves and France, by ensuring that Indochina does not fall into the hands of a hostile power during the current crisis..."

Vollenhoven cut in sharply. "If you are suggesting that it would be more advantageous for France if the Emperor of Japan snatches Indochina away from us, instead of Kaiser Wilhelm, I remain unable to see the difference. Your government is taking advantage of France's current..." he almost said, 'helplessness' then substituted another, less humiliating word, "...difficulties to annex this colony, when my government is not in a position to do anything about it."

He paused, suddenly aware that his hands were clenched in fists and his pulse was racing. He took several deep breaths before he allowed himself to continue. There was really no point in being angry with Mr. Irakawa. He was after all, a mere civil functionary who was only doing what his superiors ordered. In any event, the deed was done; the Japanese were taking over Indochina and there was nothing he or France could do about it.

A month earlier, the Japanese Consul had handed him a Note containing an ultimatum. It demanded that the French government voluntarily hand over the administration of Indochina to the representatives of the Empire of Japan, temporarily and for its own protection, naturally. Vollenhoven had immediately sent the Japanese Note on to his superiors in Paris. He had hoped that the Minister for the Colonies would tell him that a fleet of battleships and several divisions of troops were on their way to him, order him to reject the Japanese demands without qualification, and prepare to go to war in defense of France's interests. He had *hoped* for such a response, but he did not really expect it.

His lack of expectations was amply justified in the end. Under the signature of the Minister for Overseas France and its Colonies, the Honorable Albert LeBrun, came instructions which, with equivocations, reservations and meaningless bureaucratic gibberish removed, boiled down to the following:

He was ordered to defy the Japanese, to agree to nothing, and concede nothing. He was forbidden to do or say anything that would tend to impair France's claim of sovereignty over Indochina. On the other hand, he was strictly enjoined from saying anything or taking any action that might tend to provoke a military response from Japan, as the government was unable to offer him any military support in addition to the forces he presently had under his command. Within the guidelines set forth in these instructions he was to use his own best judgment. In short, he was ordered not to fight, and also not to surrender.

Certainly, fighting would be suicidal. The few thousand local soldiers led by a handful of French officers that constituted the Colonial Army were scattered all over the colony in little outposts. Even if they could be pulled together in one place, they would be utterly lacking in artillery and equipment, and without naval support. They would, moreover, be overwhelmingly outnumbered by forces that the Japanese could easily bring to bear. Under the circumstances, he had taken the only course open to him.

He waited until his pulse was steady and his voice was calm before he spoke again. He picked a sheet of paper from his desk and read from it. "Mr. Irakawa, I am authorized by my Government to state that France does not recognize the legitimacy of the forcible seizure of this colony by the Empire of Japan, that it protests this act as being contrary to both custom and international law, and states without any equivocation that, despite whatever illegal action is taken here by Japan, Indochina is and shall remain, French." He handed the official Note to the new Administrator, picked a folded newspaper from his desk with one hand, clapped his Panama hat on his head with the other, and strode briskly out of his office without a backwards glance or word of farewell.

Having been ejected from his office and his post by the Japanese, he was free of official duties for the moment. He was not sure exactly what he should do next. He wandered away from the Governor's Palace, his mind blank, with no particular destination in mind. Ten o'clock found him seated in the shade of a green-striped awning at a café on the Rue Paul Bert.

His stomach reminded him that he had not yet had breakfast, and he discovered that giving away a large section of the French Empire in a morning gave one an appetite. He ordered a *café complet,* selected a croissant from the plate of pastries brought out by the waiter, unfolded the newspaper and began to read.

The paper was the Thursday morning edition of the *Hong Kong Daily Mail*, now two days old. As Vollenhoven had discovered, since the war began the French papers had proved to be unreliable as sources of accurate information about the war. It was obvious that all the war news in the French papers was heavily censored, and since no reporters were allowed near the front, the papers were forced to rely on whatever the government gave out in their official communiqués. This meant that the French newspapers had the choice of either not writing about the war at all or reprinting the official releases, which largely consisted of descriptions of sweeping victories by France and her Russian ally that had little connection with reality.

Anyone who wanted actual information on the course of the war read the neutral papers, with the English ones generally having the best coverage. The front page headline in the *Daily Mail* was, as usual, about the war:

"Sea Battle off Cape Cepet" ran the banner in thick, black letters. In smaller type below was "Germany Claims Great Victory."

The displaced Governor General grimaced as he read the account of the battle, which had taken place a week earlier. A squadron of Royal Navy cruisers, which had been shadowing the German fleet, was able to provide eyewitness accounts of the action. The French fleet under Admiral Lapayrere had sortied out from Toulon in an attempt to break through the blockade (to go where, exactly? Vollenhoven wondered), and was met by the superior German fleet 25 kilometers southeast of Toulon (the article gave the figure in miles, and it took him a moment to convert it), commanded by Admiral Reinhard Scheer. The ensuing naval battle had raged for four hours before the French fleet, or what was left of it, withdrew back into Toulon.

The article confirmed claims out of Berlin that Scheer's fleet had sent three of the four French dreadnoughts to the bottom: *Jean Bart, France* and the fleet's flagship, *Courbet.* Based on accounts from French sailors rescued from the sea by British ships after the battle, it was estimated that over 3,000 French sailors had lost their lives as a result of the loss of the three dreadnoughts alone. The German communiqué claimed that in addition to the above, Scheer's ships had sunk three older French battleships, numerous smaller vessels, and had badly damaged the remaining French dreadnought, the *Paris*. If the information in the *Daily Mail* article was accurate, the battle had been nothing short of a catastrophe for France. The fleet had lost upwards of 5,000 sailors and three of the four most modern and powerful ships in the service. For the next few years at least, French naval power was crippled.

The official government version from Paris was that the Battle of Cape Cepet had been a French victory, and that the Germans had suffered far greater losses in both ships and men than France. No details were provided. If Vollenhoven had any doubts about which account of the sea battle to believe, this communiqué, empty of facts as it was, removed them.

He dropped the newspaper on the table and stared off into the distance. Until now, the neutral Powers had shown some restraint in not taking advantage of the war to snap up the essentially defenseless French possessions. But if Japan was going to start to gobble up French colonies in the Pacific, he thought gloomily, it seemed likely enough that other countries might start doing so too, if only to keep them out of the hands of the sticky-fingered Japanese or the voracious Germans.

Were the Americans possessively eyeing New Caledonia at this very minute? Was a Japanese fleet on its way to Tahiti as he sat here in this cafe eating pastry? He realized with a start that the entire Empire, in Asia, South America and even Africa was in danger of being lost, whether to the *boches* or others hardly mattered. The longer the war went on, the more likely it was that by its end the French Empire would have disappeared. He wondered if it was already too late to save it.

131

Chapter Thirteen: Galicia, March 17, 1915

Albert Dawson believed that he and his American Correspondent Film Company had already earned a place in the history of film (assuming such a history was ever written). He had taken his cameras closer to actual combat than anyone before had ever dared, close enough to be knocked over and splattered with mud by a shell blast while shooting footage of a French assault from a front-line German machine-gun nest in the Vosges Mountains. He was sure that no one had ever captured the reality of war in pictures more graphically than he.

But even if his earlier work was somehow overlooked or forgotten, his current project, a four-reel feature depicting the Austrian Army's attempt to recapture the fortress of Przemysl, would surely establish his place in the film industry. After this film was shown in the big theatres and new "movie palaces" and created the sensation he expected it to, he would be able to write his own ticket with the movie companies back home.

Dawson had been fascinated by photography since his senior year in high school, and had quickly discovered that he could make money shooting various outdoors scenes. Soon after graduation he began to take photographs for publication. His first assignments were for the local press in Vincennes and nearby towns in southwest Indiana and southeast Illinois. In a remarkably short time, his work came to the attention of the pioneering distributors of news photographs, Underwood and Underwood in New York. Soon, the pictures he sold them were printed all over the country.

By 1913 he had moved to Connecticut and opened his own studio. He specialized in aerial photography for real estate developers on Long Island and advertising pictures for the travel industry. In May 1913 he was hired by Matthew Clausen, publicity director of the Hamburg-America Line to photograph the maiden voyage of the SS *Vaterland*, the largest passenger liner in the world. When the war began in 1914, Claussen was hired by the German government to provide pro-German war news for American press outlets to counteract pro-Entente releases. The German government further authorized Clausen to hire American correspondents to cover the war with stories and film for release in the United States. Clausen remembered favorably the work Dawson had done for the Hamburg America Line, and offered him the assignment of filming the war from the German side.

In Berlin, he was joined by correspondent Edward Lyell Fox and a cameraman named Theyer (the man appeared to only have the one name, and Dawson was never quite sure if it was his first or last.) It was from the taciturn Theyer that Dawson learned the rudiments of motion photography. He found that he had an affinity for this kind of filmmaking, and quickly became as proficient as his teacher.

By December, the threesome were at the front in Alsace, enduring the cold rain and mud, drinking Alsatian beer and dodging shrapnel from 75mm shells fired at the German trenches by French artillery. In the months that followed, Dawson learned the trade of combat photographer under fire.

On a brief stop in Berlin before the team moved to Galicia on the Eastern Front, Dawson had been able to buy a new camera, a lightweight 35 mm Akeley "pancake", the state of the art for rugged, outdoor filmmaking. With this camera, with its three interchangeable lenses and ability to capture images in light that would be too dim for other makes, combined with his experience in war photography, Dawson felt fully prepared for the project ahead.

His new assignment was to make a four-reel feature-length "actuality film" of the forthcoming Battle of Przemysl. This fortress on the heights of the San River covered the northern approaches to the passes in the Carpathian Mountains, which sheltered the fertile Hungarian plain. Przemysl had been surrounded when the Russian offensive out of Poland in August drove Franz-Joseph's armies from Galicia. The garrison held out heroically during an epic siege that lasted for six months, before they had finally been forced to surrender in February. Now, the Russians were in retreat, and the Austrians were eager to recapture the lost fortress.

In spite of the limitations inherent in filming something so sprawling and unpredictable as a major battle, they already had been able to capture some fantastic battle footage. From no more than a half-mile away, Dawson and his new cameraman Carl Everets (Theyer had disappeared one day, without so much as a goodbye handshake) had taken dramatic shots of fortifications as they were being blasted by the heavy Austrian artillery. Their cameras recorded the effects of shells from the huge 30.5 centimeter Skoda mortars and the monstrous Krupp 420mm Big Berthas as they tore great chunks of stone, concrete and metal from the walls of the fortress. A few "shorts" from the big guns scattered sharp splinters of rock close enough to make Dawson wonder, not for the first time, why he had left peaceful Connecticut to take up such a dangerous line of work.

With correspondent Edward Fox at his side, Dawson was filming a scene of the preparations for the assault at an Austrian brigade headquarters, when the H.Q. tent took a direct hit from a Russian shell. His Akeley recorded the horrible effects of the blast, which ripped the tent open, and sent bodies and equipment flying in all directions.

Dawson found an aerodrome in a rear area and made the acquaintance of a pilot, Captain Stefan Fejes.

The amiable Fejes agreed to take the American and his camera aloft with him in the observer's seat of his Lohner scout to record the mission, locating a Russian artillery battery. After they returned to the aerodrome, Fejes marked the battery's location on a map for the artillery. They went aloft again, this time filming the destruction of the battery by the Austrian big guns from 3,000 meters above the battlefield.

Today, he expected to film the climax of the battle and (he hoped) the most exciting action of all. This was the day scheduled for the infantry assault on the fortress, which the Austrian siege mortars had largely reduced to rubble after battering it for three days.

Dawson stationed himself atop a slight rise where he had a panoramic view of both the shell-torn ground in front of the Russian-held forts and the forts themselves. The fact that his position also exposed him to Russian fire did not cross his mind at first. He was concentrating on capturing the images of thousands of Austrian soldiers climbing from their slit trenches and storming across the fields in great, gray-blue masses. Fox, who was accompanying him on the battlefield, taking notes, had prudently stayed back in a somewhat less exposed place.

"Albert, I strongly suggest that you find some decent cover before a Russian sniper finds *you*," Fox said.

Dawson began to automatically retort that he was perfectly safe, when he heard the angry whine of a rifle slug pass close by his left ear. Looking all around for the first time, he realized how dangerous his position really was. A few yards to his left was a crater left by an errant 30.5 centimeter or 440 millimeter shell. He pointed to the shell hole, called to Fox, "Over there!" and scuttled quickly into its shelter. The men cautiously peeked over the lip of the crater to assure themselves that no one was shooting at them, before Dawson resumed filming from this new, comparatively safe location.

The Austrians reached the ruins of the fort after sustaining only light casualties, and entered with bayonets fixed. Dawson decided that he needed to get a closer look. The Russians were no longer shooting anywhere near him, as the attack had moved east to the heights overlooking the San River. He tapped Fox on the shoulder, pointed at the fortress, and said, "Come on, Ed. Let's go down there."

The two men emerged from the shell hole, and moved quickly but cautiously nearer to the fighting.

By the time they had reached the nearest part of the fort, he could hear the sharp report of rifles, the screams of wounded men and shouted orders of officers and sergeants. When he judged that they had come close enough, he motioned for Fox to crouch with him behind a jagged four-foot piece of concrete that had been blasted from the walls of the works. They were afforded a view of the interior of the fortress through an archway which had once supported a roof, but now stood topless. From this vantage point they could clearly see a platoon of Austrian infantrymen working their way through the ruins of the fort.

Suddenly, they heard a rattle of a machine gun. Straight ahead, perhaps forty feet away and directly in the camera's eye, an Austrian soldier suddenly dropped his rifle, doubled over and toppled slowly to the ground. Dawson held the camera steady on the unfortunate man, recording the kicking legs, flailing arms and twitches of the head that were either the last signs of life or the first ones of its departure. He continued to hold the shot until all movement had ceased. He wondered momentarily about the man whose death he had just filmed, whether he had left a family behind, what kind of soldier he had been and what kind of man.

By nightfall the fighting was over. The fortress had fallen to the Austrians, and Dawson had completed his filming. After all the footage was compiled and edited, *The Battle and Fall of Przemysl* would be complete, and

Dawson's reputation would be assured. He wondered whether the film would make him famous, and what fame would be like. If the movie was as successful as he hoped, he was going to find out.

Chapter Fourteen: Vosges Mountains, Alsace, April 10, 1915

Lieutenant Charles de Gaulle, with his back to a granite outcropping, faced down the slope of the mountain on which he currently crouched, looking back at the way he and his platoon had come. He considered himself lucky to be alive. Most of his men had not been so fortunate. To his left and down slope, the stubby figure of his Platoon Sergeant Georges Gruyer lay face down, unmoving. Georges' rifle lay a meter in front of him, where his last convulsive movement had thrown it after he caught a machine gun bullet in the chest.

Below and on either side, de Gaulle could see other members of his platoon lying on the rocky slope in all the varied poses of death: some on their backs; some face-down like Georges; one whose head had been torn off, probably by a chunk of shrapnel; and another whose head and chest had been separated from his lower body. The Lieutenant guessed that there were now probably fewer than ten men left alive and unwounded in his platoon out of the original forty-five that had gone into the battle two days before.

They had attacked three times in three days, rushing up the slope, yelling fiercely (to frighten the waiting *boches*; de Gaulle could picture them trembling with fear in their concrete revetments), charging German positions on the side of the thickly forested mountain with the *élan* that made the Thirty-Third Regiment one of the famous fighting units of the Army. They merely confirmed what de Gaulle and other French officers in the front lines already knew, but that no-one on the General Staff understood: *élan*, guts, courage, the spirit of the offensive, call it what you will, could not overcome machine-gun bullets, nor was it protection from shrapnel sprayed by modern artillery shells.

Appropriately enough, it had been one of General Joffre's classmates at *Ecole Polytechnique* who had been the source of the disease that had eventually infected the entire French military establishment: the Doctrine of the Offensive. In the late 1880s, Captain Georges Gilbert began to preach that the only reason for France's defeat in 1870 had been the defensive mindset which allowed the Prussians to take the initiative. His idea, that the all-out attack was the solution to all military problems, the so-called "*furia francaise*," became by the late 1890s the basis for what passed for thought at the *Ecole de Guerre,* the training ground for France's future military leaders.

Gilbert's chief disciple, who elaborated his concepts into what eventually became official doctrine, was Ferdinand Foch. Foch, who quickly became the most popular instructor at the War College, taught that battle is a struggle between wills, only lost when one side believes itself beaten. What was unforgivable to de Gaulle was that Foch was fully aware of the capabilities of modern rifled small arms, machine guns and rapid-firing steel artillery, but discounted them, insisting that all of these innovations favored the bold attacker, who could "march straight onto the goal and finish the contest by means of cold steel, superior courage, and will."

In his books (de Gaulle had been impressed when read them as a cadet at Saint Cyr), Foch had sensibly insisted on the equal importance of flexibility, security and economy of force. In *Conduct of War* and *Principles of War* , Foch warned that a commander could destroy the "will to conquer" by attacking the enemy where he was strong rather than where he was weak, and that *élan* would not overcome the effects of recklessness or poor planning. These caveats were missing from his lectures, however.

Worse still, after Foch left the *Ecole de Guerre* to take a field command, he did nothing to correct the dangerously abridged versions of his teachings that were propounded by his favorite pupil and protégé, Louis de

Grandmaison. In Grandmaison's hands, Foch's ideas were simplified to the point of inanity, if not insanity. His book was filled with things like "Charge the enemy in order to destroy him... all other conceptions should be rejected as contrary to the very nature of war." Foch's emphasis on planning, preparation, security was shrugged off: "Imprudence is the best security... [victory] can be obtained only at the price of bloody sacrifice." De Gaulle had only to look at the still forms of his men on the Alsatian hillside to confirm the latter part of that statement, at least.

This kind of talk was red meat for Grandmaison's auditors, the future leaders of the French Army. In 1911, when Joffre, an enthusiastic and uncritical proponent of Grandmaison's theories, succeeded to the post of commander-in-chief, the *offensive à outrance* became the gospel for the French Army. The result was a series of new tactical field manuals for infantry and artillery, reflecting the new verities: attack was everything, defense nothing. Any officer who dared to openly disagree with this doctrine suddenly found his prospects for advancement stunted or shattered altogether.

Oddly enough, Grandmaison, Foch and Joffre had studied the effects of the combination of trenches, barbed wire, machine guns and shrapnel from quick-firing steel artillery in the Russo-Japanese War. Grandmaison had even been an observer in Siberia in 1905 and had seen the carnage wreaked by the new weapons for himself. But, since the evidence did not support the theory of the offensive, it was dismissed as irrelevant. Grandmaison and the others concluded that the Japanese and Russian infantry in those conflicts were so deficient in courage compared to the *poilu* that the examples they provided were meaningless.

A few, like de Gaulle, saw things otherwise. The chauvinistic assumption that French soldiers were braver than those of other nations was, to his mind, ludicrous. A man charging a machine gun nest over open ground was a man who would soon be shot: how brave he was had nothing to do with it. His first commanding officer, Colonel Petain (Brigadier-General Petain now, de Gaulle mentally corrected himself), understood the importance of firepower. Why didn't the General Staff?

Along with the new tactical doctrine came new, lower estimates of the size of the German Army, based not on new information, but on wishful thinking. All previous intelligence indicating that the German Army was substantially bigger than the French was disregarded, replaced by new estimates that gave the French equality or even superiority. These new assumptions swept away any excuse to retain the pre-1911 plan to stand on the defensive, with the bulk of the army positioned in the north to meet the expected German sweep through Belgium. Possessing the bravest soldiers in the world, and with numbers on her side, how could France refrain from attacking the cowardly *boches*?

Then there was political pressure. Under the terms of the military convention of the Franco-Russian Treaty of 1894, the Czar was secretly pledged to launch an attack on East Prussia at the outset of the war, even before Russia had completed her mobilization. To obtain this promise, with its attendant risks for Russia, French premier Raymond Poincare felt obliged to promise in return that his country's armies would launch an immediate offensive at the outbreak.

Out of these elements was born the ruinous Plan XVII in 1913. Since having the weight of the German invasion come through Belgium was inconvenient for the French planners, it was now assumed that the bulk of the enemy army would be concentrated along the frontier in Alsace-Lorraine. Then, if the Germans, who were outnumbered according to the new estimates, *did* try a wide swing through Belgium with their right wing, the French thrust through their center would break through the German lines, ending in the rear of the attackers, and disrupting their offensive. And, if by some strange turn of events the offensive in Lorraine did not accomplish the dislocation of the German offensive through Belgium (not that they really *were* coming that way), then the British Expeditionary Force fighting alongside the four corps of infantry of the French Fifth Army on the left wing would be more than enough to handle anything from that quarter.

As might be expected, the combination of a strategic plan that was largely based on wishful thinking and a tactical scheme that ignored the effects of modern weapons produced a catastrophe in the Battles of the Frontier. But what was worse still, these bloody repulses did not lessen the high command's faith in the *offensive à outrance.*

It must have required a great effort of will not to see the futility of the approach after the August battles, de Gaulle thought. And *that* was inexcusable. French assaults in these same mountains were cut to pieces by the heavy *boche* artillery and the prepared defenses, which seemed to feature a German machine gun nest behind every rock and fallen tree. Even the massacres of the summer (the official casualty figure was 110,000, but de Gaulle had heard that the true number, kept back to preserve civilian morale, was closer to 250,000), did not register at the top, although the men on the front lines could see what was happening clearly enough.

And so, de Gaulle's platoon, the whole Thirty-Third Regiment, and hundreds of thousands more brave *poilus* had to be sacrificed to demonstrate that one cannot overcome a machine that fires five hundred bullets a minute at a range of two kilometers with nothing more than unprotected human bodies and courage.

Although he had seen only a small part of the whole, de Gaulle had little doubt that this new offensive would prove to be as much of a blood-drenched abortion as the Battle of the Frontiers had been. The French Army had hurled its men at a well-prepared enemy, in terrain almost designed for the defender, with a bare equality or (more likely) inferiority of numbers, inferiority in firepower, and an idiotic tactical doctrine. It was hard to imagine any other result.

Looked at in purely objective terms, excessive courage was actually a military vice under such conditions: the braver the men were, the more likely it was that they would be killed to absolutely no purpose, and thus be unavailable when they were needed. That was how de Gaulle's platoon had been reduced to its current skeleton. The fighting spirit of the Thirty-Third had led them to take insane risks, and they had paid the price.

De Gaulle heard the rattling of a machine gun off in the distance, and then an echoing cry of pain. He decided that he had waited behind this boulder for new orders for quite long enough. He peeked carefully around a rock outcropping, then scuttled, bent almost double, down the slope, and back to company headquarters to see if there was a job for him, new orders, or news about how the rest of the Regiment was faring. Any of those things was preferable to spending more time hiding behind a rock.

Chapter Fifteen: Tallinn, April 22, 1915

The speeches and celebrations had gone on all day, and judging by the happy roars that continued to pour into the little café off the Raekoja Square, they seemed likely to continue throughout the night.

Ray Swing excused himself from the table he was sharing with his companion, and went to peek out the door when the crowd roared especially loudly, to see what had happened. He could not detect a cause for the momentary swell of excitement, so he shrugged and returned to his seat.

A huge crowd of Estonians filled the Square to overflowing. They sang patriotic songs, danced, waved the new blue, black and white flag of the Republic (where did they get all those flags? he wondered. Estonian independence had just been declared that morning) and guzzled bottles of liquor. From time to time, the crowd settled down for a few minutes to listen to one of their local politicians deliver a speech from one of the big windows set high up in the massive 13th century Gothic-style Town Hall overlooking the Square. But as soon as a speaker would finish (and sometimes when he merely paused to take a deep breath), the merry mob resumed its rowdy, raucous, joyous celebration.

"Quite a party, isn't it?" asked Swing's tablemate, almost shouting to make herself heard over the happy clamor. She was a tall, pretty blonde named Emma Olsen, whom Swing had met the previous day. Emma was a buyer, traveling for her father, an importer in New York City where she also lived when she was in the States. She had come to Estonia to try to make a deal with L. Knoop and Company who owned a mill on Krenholm Island near Narva. The Krenholm Mill, Emma explained to Swing, was the largest textile mill in the world, and the quality of the clothing produced there was excellent.

Swing had met Emma when he stopped in Tallinn to file some stories. He had hoped to file them earlier, but had not had a chance until the rapid German advance up the Baltic coast had paused for a few days to allow their supply train to catch up. He found that Emma was not merely decorative but was also very knowledgeable, had a sharp, inquiring mind and was fascinated by what he had seen as a reporter traveling with the German Army in the East.

"Why not?" he shouted back. After all, it *was* their Independence Day. Estonia was, as of this moment at any rate, an independent, sovereign nation. "They might as well enjoy their independence now," he said. "I don't think it's going to last very long."

She frowned thoughtfully, and then said, "Oh, you mean because of what happened in Latvia and Lithuania?"

He nodded. In the course of his journey with the advancing gray tide of the German Army, Swing had seen similar foredoomed independence celebrations before. He had also seen the outcomes.

In Lithuania, the first Baltic State to be "liberated" by the Germans, a Revolutionary Council had met in the capital Vilnius three days after the Czar's administrators had pulled out with the last Russian troops. The Council was offered a draft Act of Independence by a representative of the German Foreign Ministry. Under the terms of this Act, Lithuania would be formally declared independent of Russia, but would request a "special relationship" with Germany, in essence becoming a German client state. The Council debated the German draft, and then bravely rejected it, producing instead a Proclamation of Independence, declaring Lithuania to be a free and sovereign State.

The next day, a company of German soldiers interrupted the deliberations of the Council, which was

145

then engaged in forming an interim government in the Vilnius Town Hall. The 15 members of the Council were taken out of the hall at bayonet point and placed under arrest. An interim government in the form of a military governor appointed by the Foreign Office in Berlin took over the reins of administration in Lithuania.

In Latvia, the story was much the same. There were wild celebrations in the streets when the Latvians learned that the Russian oppressors had fled before the advancing German Army. Leaders of the Latvian independence movement had been anticipating and preparing for the Russian exodus. The People's Council of Latvia assembled in Riga even as the last of the Russian Army units was leaving the capital, and quickly passed a Declaration of Independence. They also voted on and approved a temporary Constitution, which called for free elections to a Constituent Assembly to write a permanent Constitution, with elections to be held within 30 days. Finally, they selected an interim government from among themselves. Since the People's Council had thoughtfully prepared the various Declarations, Constitutions and ministerial lists, and had selected themselves for seats on the Council in advance, they were thus able to accomplish a great deal in a remarkably short time.

Unfortunately for the People's Council, all their work was in vain. In Riga, as in Vilnius, soldiers in *feldgrau* quickly appeared to disband the interim government, cancel the elections and install an administrator chosen by Berlin. Latvian independence, like that of Lithuania, proved to have the lifespan of a mayfly.

Swing had little doubt that the same thing would soon happen here in Estonia. Kaiser Wilhelm had not sent a million soldiers all this way to free the suffering Baltic peoples from Czarist oppression; they had come to win a war, and incidentally expand the borders of the German Empire as much as possible.

146

The German tide had washed up as far as the Gulf of Riga before being brought to a halt by the harsh Russian winter. With the spring thaw, it had resumed its advance. Swing had been traveling with Hausen's Third Army since the opening of the German spring offensive, back at the beginning of April.

As they had repeatedly done since the war in the North had turned against them, the Russians had tried to make a stand, anchoring their right wing on the Gulf of Finland on one side and the northern end of Lake Peipus on the other. The southern section of the line was centered on the city of Pskov, with the defensive earthworks running south from that key road junction. The center of the whole position was shielded by the 100 kilometer length of Lake Peipus itself.

This line lasted no longer than the earlier ones had. In the north, two divisions of Kluck's First Army, escorted by a powerful squadron of warships including the dreadnought battleships *Helgoland* and *Oldenburg*, and the battlecruiser *Goeben,* with five pre-dreadnought battleships and a screen of cruisers and destroyers, made a daring surprise landing near Narva, on the Gulf of Finland, well behind the Russian lines. The 17th Century stone fort guarding the harbor was demolished by high caliber rounds from the big ships, and the city's small garrison fled without firing a shot. The Narva force attacked the Russian line from the rear in coordination with a frontal assault by the rest of the First Army. The result was the collapse of the newly formed Russian Twelfth Army, and the northern end of the Russian defensive line.

In the south, Swing witnessed a massive artillery bombardment on the Russian positions covering the approaches to Pskov. It was delivered by more than 900 guns large and small, including a dozen 420 mm Big Berthas, twenty 30.5 cm, Austrian mortars, and 156 of the new *minenwerfer*. The shelling, as heavy as any Swing had seen so far in the war, went on for a full day and night. It proved to be almost too effective, as it cratered the battlefield so heavily that the ground was nearly impassible in some places. Swing inspected the Russian positions after Hausen's men had gone through. He saw huge shell-holes alternating with piles of dirt, bits of broken machinery, dead horses and men, wagons, trees and rocks, all mixed together in an indescribable jumble. The smell of death was overpoweringly present in the air.

When the Grand Duke had chosen Lake Peipus to shield his center, he had either overlooked the fact that the lake narrowed to a width of less than two kilometers near Pnevo in the center, or had not thought the Germans capable of launching a major assault there. This proved to be a serious miscalculation. Using thousands of boats secretly gathered near the middle of the lake, and preceded by a powerful barrage, elements of the First and Second Armies, operating under Bulow, poured across the narrow neck in the middle and rapidly secured a foothold on the far side.

The Russian position was thus quickly pierced in three places almost simultaneously. To escape total disaster, Grand Duke Nicholas had been forced to order his armies to retreat precipitously once again. According to German communiqués, he was not precipitous enough; Kluck claimed to have taken more than 150,000 prisoners from the Russian Twelfth Army in the north as a result of landing at Narva and the subsequent encirclement of the unfortunate Russians trapped by the amphibious landing.

The Russian Army was still suffering from the aftereffects of the catastrophic opening campaign in East Prussia, where the greater part of two field armies of trained veterans had been swallowed whole by the Germans. The Grand Duke had been able to call up enough reserves to form new armies and make good the losses in a purely numerical sense, but the fighting spirit of these replacements, many of whom were only half-trained and without weapons, was far lower than that of the men who been lost back in August in East Prussia. Swing had learned about the deterioration of the Russians' combat effectiveness from the Germans interrogation of prisoners and from talking to some of the prisoners himself. He had also seen with his own eyes that the Czar's soldiers no longer fought with the same stubborn courage they had displayed earlier in the war.

"You were there," Emma said. "You saw the German attack at Pskov, and a lot of other battles too, I guess. What's it like? Were you afraid?"

Swing shook his head. "I suppose a few shells landed nearby, but I never really thought I was in danger. The Russians have been taking it on the chin since the war started, and they haven't managed to do much damage to the Germans." He took another swallow of beer and grimaced. "But I can't imagine what it must have been like in the Russian trenches during the bombardment. After the attack went through, I looked around at the Russian front line positions. It was like some kind of nightmare butcher's shop, with bodies and pieces of bodies, arms and legs, scattered all over the place..." He stopped. "I'd rather not talk about it, if you don't mind."

Emma shivered. "Of course not, Ray. I understand. I'm sorry I brought it up." She patted his hand comfortingly.

Another experience he had no intention of sharing with Emma was his first look at one of the new German weapons. It was during the fighting outside Pskov that Swing finally saw in action the flamethrower about which he had heard so many rumors.

The advance of a regiment of Bavarian Grenadiers was being held up by a stubbornly defended concrete pillbox that overlooked a key road junction. The Russians had already driven back two attempts to close with them and take the strongpoint with hand grenades,

149

the Bavarians leaving little piles of bodies behind after each try. The regimental C.O., a colonel, came up in person to see what was holding up the advance, and then sent a messenger back to his headquarters.

Soon, a soldier with a strange device strapped on his back trotted up. The device consisted of a large metal cylinder three feet long and a foot in diameter, with a hose connected to a long, slender tube running from the bottom. There was a tiny flame flickering on the end of the tube, which the soldier held in his hand. The colonel personally spoke to the new man, although Swing was not close enough to hear what was said. The colonel repeatedly pointed at the pillbox, and the soldier nodded several times.

The Germans organized another attack, this time leapfrogging forward in alternation, approaching the pillbox from an angle to the right and maintaining a steady fire as they advanced. As cautiously as they advanced, several of the attackers were still hit by fire from the Russian Maxim in the pillbox. The colonel chose what he thought was the right moment, and then signaled to the soldier wearing the metal cylinder. The man ran forward heavily, angling to the left of the Russian position.

Evidently, the attack from the right side had been sufficient to draw the Russians' attention and allow the soldier get to within 15 yards of the pillbox without being seen and fired upon. He reached over his shoulder and pulled a lever on the top of the cylinder, then aimed the end of the tube at the slit in the pillbox. A long sheet of liquid flame shot out of the nozzle, accompanied by a thick cloud of greasy, black smoke. The smoke had a very unpleasant smell, something like burning rubber combined with kerosene.

A moment after the flames entered the slit in the front of the pillbox, Swing heard the occupants' screams of agony. They were the most horrifying sounds he had ever heard. To Swing, it seemed as if the screams went

150

on forever as the soldier operating the device continued to play the flames over the opening.

Then he heard a faint *clang,* and the cylinder on the flamethrower operator's back suddenly exploded, coating the German in an orange blanket of fire. A Russian bullet had found the fuel tank of the flamethrower. The soldier, burning like a torch, shrieked in unbearable anguish and spun to the ground. There was a new smell now mixing with the petroleum odor, an overpowering stench of badly scorched meat. Swing dropped to the ground on his hands and knees and vomited. He was not alone. The smell of burning flesh added to the hideous death of the flamethrower man was enough to make several of the German soldiers, veterans all, bring up the contents of their stomachs.

Swing shuddered and put aside the memory, returning his attention to the infinitely more pleasant company of Emma Olsen.

"I'm so glad our country has kept out of this idiotic war," she said.

Swing nodded his agreement. "I don't have a lot of use for Wilson; I went for Debs last time. But I will give him credit for having enough sense to stay out of this bloody mess over here." He took another long swallow from his mug.

"Anyway," he said, replacing the beer mug on the table, "probably the worst consequence of the Battle of Lake Peipus for the Russians wasn't the loss of territory, equipment, or even men," Swing said. "It was the announcement by the Czar a week after the battle that he was relieving Grand Duke Nicholas as Commander of the Russian armies and personally taking command."

"Why was that so bad?" Emma asked. "I didn't hear anybody touting Grand Duke Nicholas as the second coming of Robert E Lee. The Russians have been getting their heads beaten in since the war started. How much worse could the Czar be?"

"I haven't spoken to a single military man or reporter whose opinion I trust who thinks that the Czar's decision wasn't a colossal blunder," Swing answered. He took another long gulp of his beer, and explained.

"Whatever you might think about the military abilities of the Grand Duke (and I don't have a very high opinion of them), he is at least a soldier, trained in handling large numbers of men and planning battles for big, modern armies. Czar Nicholas the Second, on the other hand, has absolutely no practical military experience or training, unless you want to count sitting on a horse reviewing parades, and on top of that is reputed to have a generally mediocre intelligence at best. Even if by some miracle it turned out that the Czar was natural military genius on the order of a Lee or Napoleon, it would still take time for him to master the complexities of managing an army of millions of men on a front stretching thousands of miles. Russia doesn't have time for the Supreme Commander of its armed forces to learn on the job."

"Well then, I suppose that he would just let the best general he had left tell him what to do, at least until he figured out which end of the stick to grab, and pretend to give the orders himself," she said.

Swing shook his head. "That would normally be the right thing to do, but there really isn't anybody on the Russian General Staff that he can count on," he replied. He signaled the bartender for another round. "You want one?" he asked. She nodded.

"Where was I?" he asked.

"The Czar can't count on his General Staff..." she prompted.

"Oh yeah... thanks," he said to the bartender who had returned with two foaming mugs. He took a long pull at his beer. "Say, you should forget about importing wool socks from that L. Knoop and Company. What your father *should* import is this Saku Beer. It's better than anything we have back Chicago."

152

"It is good," she agreed. "So, what is the problem with the Russian General Staff?"

Swing set the mug down on the table. "Although the Russians have a few competent generals, like Brusilov and Dmitriev, on the whole, the highest levels of the Russian military establishment are notable for their incompetence and corruption. Rank is mostly based on nobility of birth, political connections and talent for intrigue. Few officers of real ability are permitted to rise in the Czarist system, because they might endanger the positions of the entrenched incompetents..."

"Which goes a long way toward explaining the course of the war here in the East," she finished for him. Swing nodded, impressed again by her quick understanding. "The Czar doesn't have any half-way competent general to lean on while he tries to learn how to be Commander-in-Chief. There aren't any."

"None that he can trust, anyway. The Czar has to rely on the very small circle of people he *can* trust, which basically limits him to his relatives," Swing said. "The Grand Duke might not be the most brilliant general in the world, but..."

"He is the Czar's first cousin, so at least his loyalty isn't an issue," Emma finished.

Swing nodded. "The Czar is probably going end up relying on advice from his wife and whatever religious charlatan is currently in favor at the Court," he said. "I'm pretty sure they aren't going to be able to give him the kind of help he will need."

In his article on the sacking of the Grand Duke, Swing had written that the Czar's move was equivalent to another major defeat for Russia, equal to the one suffered in August in East Prussia. The German First Army was now at Narva, a little more than 100 miles from St. Petersburg, gathering supplies and preparing for the final spring to the Russian capital. Time was definitely running out for the Czar and his empire.

"To make matters worse," Swing continued, "the Ministry of War is said to be rotten from top to bottom, with the possible exception of the Minister himself, Sukhomlinov. So the Russian Army's not even getting a lot of the supplies that *are* available, things like small arms ammunition and food, because they're being siphoned off by Ministry bureaucrats for their personal profit. In my opinion, if God Himself took command He wouldn't be able to save the Czar."

After taking another long swallow from her mug, Emma asked, "Do you have any news about what's going on with the rest of the war? I can't find an English or American paper that's less than a week old around here."

"There's a little news stand on the other side of the Square where you can get the *Daily Mail*, two days old. Got one right here," Swing said, bringing it up from the seat next to him and shaking it open. Emma leaned in, pressing close to Swing in an attempt to read the paper over his shoulder by the inadequate light of an overhead wagon-wheel candelabra.

"Looks like more bad news for France and Russia," Swing said, squinting at the newsprint and trying not to let Emma's near presence distract him. "Down in the Black Sea, those two new dreadnoughts the Brits built for Turkey have been cruising around sinking every Russian ship they find, and blowing up the port facilities and oil processing plants at Sevastopol. The Russian Baltic Fleet has nothing to match those monsters." He turned a page.

"Here's something interesting," he said. "It's a report on the Turkish invasion of the Caucasus over the winter. They finally have a reliable account of what happened. It was a disaster for the Turks. The weather did most of the fighting for the Russians. The article estimates that blizzards froze a hundred thousand Turkish soldiers to death."

Balanced against this success was a calamity for the Entente's sole ally in the Balkans, Serbia. The Germans had brought Rumania and Bulgaria into the Triple Alliance with offers of Serbian territory once the conquest of the little nation was accomplished. Their armies had joined the Austrian Third Army and the German Eleventh to overrun Russia's ally in a three-week campaign, crushing the Serbian Army and forcing the Serbs to surrender on April 18.

The Serbian government had been accused of involvement in the conspiracy that assassinated the heir to the Hapsburg throne, Archduke Francis Ferdinand by the Austro-Hungarian Empire. This incident had started the war when Austria-Hungary declared war on Serbia in July 1914, and Serbia's ally Russia supported her with a declaration of war against the Dual Monarchy. Serbia was out of the war and was probably soon to be erased from the map.

"What about the Western Front?" Emma asked. "The last I read, the French had launched their big spring offensive and were predicting that they would be in Berlin by Bastille Day."

"They've been hammering away at the Germans in the Vosges Mountains for three weeks now," Swing replied. He scanned the front page article in the *Daily Mail* about the French offensive. "The French are saying that everything is proceeding on right on schedule and exactly as planned. They also claim to have inflicted enormous casualties on the Germans in the fighting in Alsace-Lorraine. The war correspondent for the *Daily Mail,* Basil Clarke, says that he has been unable to confirm any of these reports."

"They're allowing foreign reporters at the front now?" Emma asked, surprised.

Swing grinned cynically. "The credibility of the official communiqués sank so low that the French had to allow a few foreign reporters up to the front. It got so bad that if the French government communiqué had announced that the sun was going to rise in the East, everybody would have started looking for it come up in the West." He looked at the paper again. "Even the official dispatches out of Paris admit that the front has advanced no deeper than ten kilometers into the German lines anywhere. They're not claiming any significant territorial gains."

Swing had traveled in Alsace and Lorraine before the war. The land was rugged, the woods were thick and the roads were few and narrow. It was a defender's dream. He had no doubt that the Germans had spent the winter stringing up barbed wire and building strong points, machine gun nests, pillboxes, and artillery positions in preparation for the French spring offensive. Rapid offensive movement in Alsace was practically impossible, and any ground gained there could come only at heavy cost to the attackers.

"I've seen that country where the French are trying to break through," Swing said. "If you want my opinion, this whole spring offensive is going to be a repeat of the Battle of the Frontiers of last summer, when the French Army lost a quarter-million men trying to butt head-first through a stone wall."

"Hold on. There is a small ray of sunshine for the French," Swing said, turning a page. "They managed to throw back an Italian invasion in the mountains north of Nice."

"Was that a surprise, that the French beat the Italians, I mean?" Emma asked.

"Not really," Swing answered, "for two reasons. First, the terrain there is even more difficult for armies than Alsace-Lorraine is. The Alps in that region are practically impassible if they are defended at all. Second, the Italian Army is probably the least efficient one in Western Europe, and might even rate lower than Turkish levies in actual combat."

Swing finished off his beer with one long swallow, rose from the table, and extended his hand. "Well, I wish I didn't have to say this, but I have to shove off. It's been great meeting you, Emma. It is an unexpected pleasure to run into a fellow American over here, especially one as pretty and as sharp as you. Next time I get to New York, I'll look you up. Anyway, I have to get out to the front early tomorrow morning. I think the Germans are going to make another big push, and I'm going to have to be there to cover it. So, I'm for bed. Good night."

Emma ignored the proffered hand. She rose and emptied her mug. She set it down on the table with a thump. "Say, that's a coincidence," she said, "I was about to go to bed, too. Suppose I join you?"

Swing smiled as he thought about the agreeable surprises travel to foreign lands can sometimes bring. "That sounds like a fine idea. It would be a shame to waste a good coincidence, wouldn't it?" Swing suspected that he would be one tired pup at dawn when he left for the battlefield, but that thought did not keep him from smiling as he walked from the bar into noisy night of Old Town Tallinn, with Emma Olsen on his arm.

The Austrian private, 1915

Secretary of State William Jennings Bryan
(*not* the Wonderful Wizard of Oz)

President Woodrow Wilson thinking great thoughts

Young man on the make:
Assistant Secretary of the Navy, Franklin D. Roosevelt,

A T-51 Baldwin locomotive, circa 1912

Governor-General Joost van Vollenhoven in uniform

Palace of the Governor-General of Indochina, Hanoi

Battle Line of the High Seas Fleet, 1914

Pride of the French Navy: Battleship *Jean Bart*

Fortress Przemsyl after bombardment, 1915

Lieutenant Charles DeGaulle hearing Destiny calling

General Ferdinand Foch with a demonstration of *elan*

Raekoja Square, Old Town Tallinn

Another triumph of modern science:
French flamethrowers, 1915

German field artillery moving up, Galicia, 1915

Lohner B VII Scout with pilot and observer

German cavalry with pointed sticks, 1914

Austrian field works in Galicia, 1915

Napoleon Bonaparte reincarnated:
Czar Nicholas II takes command

The man he replaced:
Grand Duke Nicholas

First Lord of the Admiralty Winston Churchill
eyeing the threat across the North Sea

Chapter Sixteen: Near Lemberg May 3, 1915

Captain Stefan Fejes never regretted his decision to leave the Imperial Cavalry and join the Royal and Imperial Aviation Corps, in spite of the fact that he had seemed destined for a career in the cavalry. His grandfather had been an officer in the cuirassiers, and had fought for the Empire in the victorious wars of 1859 (against the French), 1864 (against the Danes) and in the calamity of 1866 against the Prussians. Arpad Fejes had retired with several medals, a colonel's pension and a wooden leg.

His father been a Captain in the peacetime cavalry, and regularly lamented that he never had a chance to lay his sabre on the head of one of the Emperor's enemies in combat. To Stefan, however, the prospect of wearing gilded body armor while leading a squadron of lancers in a cavalry charge was not romantic. To his way of thinking, it was an idiotic vestige of a bygone era. The age of fighting from horseback had passed and gone, or it would have, if hidebound old generals still preparing for the Napoleonic Wars would let it. Fifteen years into the Twentieth Century, the Imperial cavalry still carried lances into battle, *lances,* as if the age of the armored knight was still in flower. Of what use, he wondered, was a pointed stick on the modern battlefield? A mounted man was just a big, slow-moving target for rifles and machine guns, to say nothing of what shrapnel would do to a man sitting exposed on horseback two meters off the ground.

The last legitimate military justification for cavalry was reconnaissance work. Light cavalry had long ago proved its worth by scouting for the mass of infantry and driving off the enemy cavalry, and keeping them from monitoring your army's movements. But the rapid development of heavier-than-air aviation technology (and this also applied to dirigible airships) had rendered the scouting function of the cavalry arm obsolete as well. One man in an aeroplane could gather more intelligence, cover more ground in a single day, than an entire regiment of mounted troops could in a week.

The speed and modernity of flight had an irresistible attraction for him. Fejes had fallen in love with the aeroplane the first time he saw one at a fair outside Budapest in 1907. He ignored his father's outraged disapproval of his new interest, spending all of his free time and practically all of his disposable income on flying lessons. When the Royal Balloon Corps was renamed the Royal and Imperial Aviation Corps, it began to buy aeroplanes for military use and called for volunteers with flying experience. Fejes almost broke his arm in his hurry to fill out an application for a transfer to the new Corps.

His C.O. made a sour face when he signed on Fejes' transfer. "You're going to regret this some day, young man. Aeroplanes will never be any of practical value in warfare."

Fejes saw no point in debating the issue with the crusty old Colonel, but he harbored not the slightest doubt that the cavalry, sabre, lance, cuirass and all the rest, would soon join the Egyptian chariot squadron, the Greek phalanx and the Balearic slingshot corps on the dust-heap of military history.

Conversely, aerial warfare was still in its infancy, and its future prospects were unlimited. In 1911, the year before Fejes joined Aviation, the Frenchman Edouard Nieuport had set a speed record by flying at more than 140 kilometers per hour, which Fejes found amazing. His own machine, a Lohner B. VII, had a comparatively low top speed of 115 km per hour after it was fueled up and loaded with pilot and observer. Even so, it was a lot faster than a horse.

171

There were certain days, like today, when Fejes remembered all over again how happy he was to be out of Cavalry and in Aviation. As he flew over the battlefield, looking down at the unfortunate foot soldiers who had to fight it out in the mud, he thanked whatever gods there were that he was up *here* and not down *there*. Even seen from the considerable height of three thousand meters, the battlefield looked like a suburb of Hell.

The big offensive had started three days earlier. The Russians had been steadily stripping troops from this part of the front and sending them north to try to stem the German advance along the Baltic. Someone on the General Staff had finally realized that the Russian front, from roughly Seydlets east of Warsaw in the north, to Czernowitz in the south, was likely to be thinned out and vulnerable. Moltke in Berlin had shipped the Ninth, Tenth and Eleventh Armies down to Galicia, sandwiching them in between the Austrian First, Second, Third and Fourth Armies, building up to over a million men altogether, and put the whole operation under General August von Mackensen. They brought in an enormous number of guns, both German and Austrian to put some real muscle into the attack. Fejes estimated that there were over a thousand guns of all sorts in his sector alone, from the big 30.5 centimeter and 21 centimeter heavies, through the 15 centimeter field howitzers, down to the 105 millimeter and 7.7 centimeter field pieces.

After two days of pounding the Russian positions, the preliminary bombardment for the assault began just after sunrise at 05:10 hours, with a roar that sounded like the end of the world. He could not imagine what conditions were like on the receiving end in the Russian trenches. He did not try very hard.

But he was to find out soon enough. Two hours after sun-up, the squadron leader ordered the wing aloft to observe the effects of the bombardment. Fejes and his

172

observer, a young Lieutenant named Weiss, pulled on their leather flying jackets, gloves and helmets (it got pretty cold up at three thousand meters, even in May), and climbed up into their seats on the Lohner, and watched their ground crew spin the prop and get the engine started. In a few minutes, they were spiraling up over the field.

Fejes was in no hurry to head out over no-man's land until he had gained enough altitude to be reasonably sure that one of his side's howitzers did not accidentally put a shell through the plane. Finally, when he reached three thousand meters, he felt safe enough to level off and swing east toward the Russian lines, with the shells whistling by underneath them.

Fejes had been over the Russian lines daily for weeks before the opening of the battle, and had practically memorized every feature of the defenses for a hundred kilometers north and south, all the way back to their third line. The Russian defensive system was not very elaborate. In many places, it consisted of earthen walls built up to about 5 meters in height, backed by trenches to shelter the riflemen. The line lacked the usual protective sandbag parapets; machine gun nests were few and far between; there were hardly any concrete, stone or even wood-reinforced strong points; and even that most basic element of modern defensive warfare, the ubiquitous concertinas of barbed wire, looked thin and inadequate.

Now though, after two days under this tremendous artillery pounding, the Russian positions were almost unrecognizable. In the place of a continuous line that looked from above like a long worm cut, there remained only a few severed, isolated segments of the trenches. Large sections of the Russian front line works had simply disappeared, buried under great piles of loose earth or obliterated by gaping craters. Weiss patted his shoulder and pointed. A shell from one of the heavy guns, a big howitzer perhaps, made a direct hit on one of the few strongpoints in the Russian line, a concrete-reinforced artillery observation post on a little hill. There was an enormous blast, and a billowing black cloud, and he saw great chunks of concrete tumbling end over end high in the air, alongside other smaller bits, some of which he was sure were men, or pieces of them.

Everywhere below, great geysers of earth were being flung heavenward by the explosions. The few Russian soldiers he saw were running towards the rear, trying to escape the hellish shelling.

Flying deeper into Russian territory, Fejes could see that there was no safety for the Czar's men further back. Shells were also crashing into the second line and behind it, disrupting the rear areas, blasting the communication trenches that zigzagged up to the forward zone and keeping any reinforcements from reaching the front line.

Five kilometers behind no-man's-land, he passed over what had been a Russian artillery park. The big Austrian and German siege mortars had zeroed in on the coordinates of these guns (largely thanks to information provided by Fejes and his flying brothers, he thought with satisfaction), and their huge shells had reduced the Russian batteries to an open-air abattoir. Scattered all around, like a careless child's toys, were broken guns and bits of guns, with many of their crews lying motionless beside them on the churned-up earth.

His B.VI may not have been the fastest aeroplane ever made, but it had phenomenal endurance. Fejes had heard stories of Lohners staying aloft for as long as six hours straight without refueling, although he would not have cared to push it that far. He was very comfortable staying airborne for four hours at a stretch, though. So, he was still circling at 3000 meters, continuing to observe the effects of the bombardment when, at exactly 09:10, the big guns fell silent.

He heard the roar of a hundred thousand men over the growl of the B.VI's 150-horsepower Daimler engine, as waves of gray-blue Austrian and *feldgrau* German storm troops clambered out of their trenches and moved into no-man's-land. He was flying right over the boundary between the German Tenth and the Austrian First Armies, so that the Germans were advancing under his left wing and the Austrians under his right.

The attacking waves crossed to the Russian positions (what was left of them, anyway) almost without opposition in most places. Here and there, a machine gun nest or strongpoint would provide a momentary check in some small area of the advancing tide, but these islands of resistance were quickly surrounded and neutralized by small detachments from the swarms of attackers. The attack went on through to the Russian second line almost without a pause.

Here, relatively more of the defensive positions were still intact, and what did remain was manned by riflemen who continued to shoot at the advancing gray waves until they were either killed by bullets, grenades or bayonet attacks, or surrounded and forced to surrender. By the time Fejes decided to return to the aerodrome to refuel, the Russians were still holding the third and final line, but it did not appear that they would be able to do so for very long.

He ate a hurried meal with one hand (sausage and potato salad again, although he hardly noticed what he was eating), while writing a report of his observations with the other hand. He wanted to get aloft again as soon as possible, and was mightily annoyed when he discovered that the ground crew had not even refueled his machine by the time he had finished his meal and returned to the airfield.

However, after a few barked orders and some scrambling around by the ground crew, he and Weiss were in the sky again a few minutes later. He had a feeling that something big was about to break, and he wanted to be there to see it.

If the first two lines of the Russian defenses were inadequate, the third line was far weaker still. There was hardly any wire, and virtually no built-up strong points to shelter the defenders' trench mortars and machine gun crews. Fejes was aware of this from his many previous scouting flights, and he was convinced that if the first line two lines collapsed, the third would be swept away like a twig in a flood. He supposed that General Mackensen would want to keep up the pressure, and would order his commanders to quickly reorganize the assault teams, bring up the reserves, lay on another preliminary bombardment and renew the attack to create a clean breach through the Russian line while there was still plenty of daylight to exploit the breakthrough.

They floated over the cratered beet fields (there would be a poor harvest this year for the local farmers) for two hours, as the German and Austrian heavy guns reduced the final Russian defensive position to a chaotic scramble of mud, men and weapons. When the guns fell quiet, a renewed tide of Teutonic soldiers poured out of the captured Russian trenches. Almost as soon as the attackers emerged, he saw a trickle of the brown-clad defenders fleeing their line and running east. As the attacking force drew closer, the trickle became a flood composed of thousands of Russian soldiers throwing away rifles, packs, and anything else that could encumber them, fleeing the battlefield as fast as their legs could carry them. Many thousands more emerged from their trenches with their hands held high as the troops reached their positions.

These were clearly not the same Russian soldiers who had fought so well back in August, when they had thrown back the Austrian Army's opening offensive out of Galicia, and had come close to surrounding and annihilating three of the four invading Austrian field armies. These, the Russian infantry of May 1915, were beaten men. Fejes did not think that anything short of a miracle could rally them.

Three days later, he had still not seen anything to prove him wrong. The armies advanced into a vacuum along most of the front, marching forward twenty-five kilometers a day against practically no opposition. A few isolated Russian units put up fierce resistance: in the town of Sandomierz, an entire corps dug in and fought for two days until they ran out of ammunition and were forced to surrender. But, for the most part, it seemed that the Russian Army had ceased to exist as an organized fighting force in this part of Poland. Fejes had heard about the great victories won by the Germans up north; it was apparent that the Russians were losing everywhere. He wondered if the war in the East was nearly over.

Chapter Seventeen: London, May 23, 1915

The Honorable Winston Spenser Churchill glowered down at the bundle of newspapers, and then swung his head up to fix his baleful glare on the Lieutenant who had just delivered them, as if whatever was troubling the First Lord of the Admiralty was somehow the fault of the young officer.

"How is it," he growled, "that the private news journals are in a position to obtain essential military information more promptly than His Majesty's Government?" he demanded, slapping the pile of newspapers with the back of his hand, and sending cigar ash flying.

The Lieutenant stammered, "Why... I don't know, sir... I suppose..."

Churchill did not wait to hear the young officer's answer to a question that had not, in truth, been directed at him. "Never mind," he interrupted. He motioned with his cigar. "You are dismissed. Remain within earshot just outside that door," he cautioned the aide, quite unnecessarily. Churchill's regular man was out attending a sick relative today, and the First Lord was suspicious of any changes in his staff. The Lieutenant saluted, and slipped silently out the door.

The truth was that Churchill was not nearly so displeased by the fact that the news media had "scooped" the official British government sources (he had no quarrel with the press in general, having started his career in public life as a war reporter), as by the news itself. He picked up the *Sunday Times* from the stack. The lead story was "Russians Ask for Armistice," and below in smaller type was written "Fighting to Cease at 12:00 P.M., 26 May." Gloomily, he read the article that followed.

The German-Austrian offensive in Galicia that had begun at the in May had resulted in the rapid disintegration of the Czar's armies on the southern half of the front. The Russian soldiers did not simply retreat; many apparently made up their minds that the war was over, and had gone home for good. For three weeks, the Teutonic armies had advanced through Poland and the Ukraine with virtually no resistance. *The Times* reported that, as had happened elsewhere, the invaders were greeted by cheering crowds, flowers, and kisses from the local women. The Czar's government was evidently no more popular in Poland and the Ukraine than it had been in Latvia, Lithuania, Estonia or Finland.

In the north, the Germans had approached to within fifty kilometers of St. Petersburg. In this sector, so near to the capital, the Russian soldiers were still willing to fight, even if not very effectively. Nevertheless, it was clear that if the Czar's government had not asked for an armistice, St. Petersburg would have fallen in a matter of weeks, possibly even days. While the lines had stabilized in the north after the cease-fire agreement had been reached, in the south the German, Austrian, and Rumanian armies continued to advance as rapidly as they could, trying to occupy as much Russian territory as possible before the cease-fire took effect.

He put *The Times* aside to pick up the *Daily Mirror*. "Demonstrations in St. Petersburg" was the headline there. The subheading was "Calls from Duma for Czar to Abdicate." Churchill shook his head as he read the story, frowned, and unconsciously made a low, rumbling noise deep in his throat. It was the Revolution of 1905 all over again, except that this time the scope of the disaster was far greater, and the probability that Nicholas II would be able to retain his throne was too small to consider.

The First Lord considered it unlikely that even the Czar's immediate abdication would be sufficient to save the Romanovs. Churchill had little doubt that the terms of the peace treaty the Germans would impose on their defeated foes would be so harsh as to doom the dynasty. The Germans would undoubtedly either annex vast regions of the Ukraine, Poland, Belorussia and the Baltic States that they currently occupied, or else establish "independent" states there that would be German dependencies in practice. When the Czar (whoever it was by then) agreed to such terms, as he would have to do, Churchill could not see how the Russian monarchy could long survive the effects of signing such a humiliating and catastrophic treaty.

Nothing about this war had gone the way the First Lord of the Admiralty had wanted, ever since the Kaiser had inexplicably called off the invasion of Belgium and turned his armies against Russia. It had been, in fact, an embarrassing misadventure for Churchill and the rest of the small group of cabinet members and military men who had worked for closer ties with France, and had hoped to join the British Empire to the Franco-Russian Entente. All their preparations, all their plans for the coming war, had been based on assumption that the Germans would violate Belgian neutrality.

When that did not happen, they were left stranded high and dry, helpless to affect the outcome of the greatest and most momentous war in a century. Here Churchill had command of the most powerful navy in the world, and he could do nothing but watch as the fleets of the parvenu German Empire went blithely about, shelling and blockading the helpless French ports, seizing or sinking French shipping, turning neutral merchantmen back from France, and generally carrying on as though *they*, rather than the British Empire, were the heirs to four centuries of naval tradition. How he longed to pick up the telephone and order Admiral Jellicoe to take the Battle Line down into the Channel to clear away the German blockaders with a few well-placed rounds of 13 1/2 inch armor-piercing shell! He gritted his teeth in frustration.

He remembered lingering after a cabinet meeting in late August to talk with Lord Kitchener, shortly after it became clear that the Germans were not going to invade Belgium, and that as a consequence, His Majesty's Government was not going to enter the war. Churchill had asked the Secretary of State for War for his estimate of the Franco-Russian Entente's prospects in the coming conflict.

"They have no chance at all without us," Kitchener had responded almost immediately. "I should imagine that the French will be able to carry on for a while, but the Russians won't last more than a year." Churchill, Grey and the other pro-French members of the Cabinet had since come to see this dismal forecast borne out by events.

The British Empire now faced a grim post-war prospect. A bloated German Empire (and its Austro-Hungarian ally) would undoubtedly either annex or control through new puppet states most of the productive farmland, iron ore and coalfields of the Ukraine, Belorussia and southern Poland, together with the rich Baltic coastal lands from Lithuania to Estonia. Together, the Teutonic Powers would dominate Europe militarily and economically; a crippled Russia, with its most prosperous and productive provinces lopped off (and possibly having suffered through a civil war?) would be far too weak for many years to provide any sort of counter-weight.

The Mediterranean Sea was, for all practical purposes, already a Triple Alliance lake. Since being savaged at Cape Cepet, the French fleet was no longer a factor. The Mediterranean Squadron of the Royal Navy was in no position to challenge the Austrian-Italian-German Allied Fleet, should some future crisis bring about a confrontation. The Suez Canal, that vital artery through which flowed the commerce that was the lifeblood of the Empire, would be a hostage to the German-dominated constellation.

181

Churchill believed that Great Britain's best hope in that region would in the diplomatic realm. It would require nothing short of a miracle to keep ancient enemies, Austria, Italy and Turkey yoked together in the same alliance system for very long. Britain should be able to detach at least one of them, probably Italy. He scribbled a reminder to himself to brace Grey about at the next Cabinet meeting.

And what, he wondered, would the Kaiser demand from France as the price of peace? Would the Germans offer to negotiate, or simply transfer the million and a half fighting men from the now quiescent Eastern Front to the West, and break through the French fortress system with the overwhelming weight of men and metal? The French would charge a high price in German lives, but if the Kaiser wanted to add Paris to his conquests, Churchill did not see any way he could be stopped.

Chapter Eighteen: Berlin, June 29, 1915

Helmuth von Moltke unconsciously fingered the gleaming head of his brand-new *Generalfeldmarschall*'s baton as he stood in the Kaiser's map room of the Stadtschloss, awaiting his sovereign. He recalled his last visit to the royal palace, back in August, when he had come very near to being sacked for disputing war strategy with the Kaiser. In retrospect, he was forced to admit that the Kaiser's order to turn the Army east against the Russians had proved to be the correct one. It was hard to see how the war could have gone much better for Germany had the invasion of Belgium proceeded as originally planned, and easy to see how it could have gone very much worse.

Moltke was secretly (very secretly) embarrassed to be the object of the great popular adulation that followed the victory over the Russians, when he well knew that the Kaiser's rash decision (he *still* believed it was rash) was the primary reason for the favorable outcome of the war. His promotion to Field-Marshal only made his embarrassment worse. To cover his unease, he gazed down at his Prussian Field Marshal's baton, studying it as though the secrets of the universe were inscribed on it.

The baton was certainly a garish object. It was a meter long, capped by a ruby-encrusted golden knob. The sovereign's name was inscribed in tiny letters in the scrollwork under the cap, and the blue velvet-covered shaft was encrusted with crowns alternating with eagles, all worked in gold, of course. Objectively speaking, it was one of the ugliest things he had ever seen. But what it represented was the culmination of any professional soldier's career.

While Moltke was musing, the Kaiser arrived, his medals clinking and his ceremonial sword bouncing against his thigh as he approached. The Field Marshal was also in his full dress uniform, of which the baton was a part, since in less than an hour he was to stand by the side of his monarch as the first of the victorious armies returning from the East passed in review down the Unter den Linden.

Moltke clicked his heels, bowed and stood stiffly to attention.

"I grant you permission to sit in my presence," said the Kaiser, smiling, and motioning for him to sit on a brocaded Empire sofa. He glanced down at the baton, then up at Moltke.

"Are you perhaps a little uncomfortable with your promotion?" he asked shrewdly. Before he could reply, Wilhelm went on, "I can assure you, my dear Field Marshal, that no-one has ever deserved the honor more than you. The way you improvised the campaign in East Prussia, indeed, your entire handling of the war, has been masterful. Accept the honors I have given you, and be content in the knowledge that you have served your Emperor and your country well."

"Yes, well, thank you, then, Your Majesty, you are very gracious," Moltke replied, abashed. "I will try to do as you say."

"Good," returned the Kaiser. "But I had a particular reason for bringing you here a little early for the review. You must have heard that I trust the advice of my generals more than that of my ministers."

There was one time at least when you declined to follow my advice, Moltke thought, but he said only, "Yes, Your Majesty, I was aware of it."

"I wish to hear your views on a matter which is not wholly military in nature," the Kaiser continued. "First, how many men would it cost us to prosecute the war against France until she would be driven to her knees and forced to surrender?"

"A repeat of 1871, including taking Paris, I suppose?" Moltke asked, referring to the war in which the Kaiser's grandfather army had humbled the legions of Napoleon III.

"Yes, precisely," Wilhelm agreed.

The Field Marshal stared up at the gilded ceiling for a few moments, his lips moving silently. "To penetrate the Belfort to Verdun fortress line might cost 400,000 to a half-million casualties over four to six months. After that, perhaps as many again to destroy the French field armies and occupy Paris, and considerably more if Paris is defended. Street fighting in cities can be very bloody."

The Kaiser pursed his lips and frowned. "I thought it might be something like that. Holstein and Jagow…" (the Chancellor and Foreign Minister, respectively, for whose military opinions Moltke had not the slightest regard) "…insist that we must crush the French so that they can never rise to challenge us again. I would not be surprised if they want to permanently occupy France, or perhaps annex it to the Reich." Wilhelm shook his head at the thought. "Now another military question for you: do you believe that the French Army is a serious danger to Germany, or that it will be in the next decade?"

"That is an easier one to answer, Your Majesty," Moltke replied immediately. "Unless she gains some formidable allies, France is impotent to harm us, and I expect that to be true for many years to come."

The Kaiser nodded. "That confirms my own opinion," he said. "Now we come to the question which is perhaps outside of your area of expertise. The American President, Wilson, has offered to mediate a peace between ourselves and France. I intend to accept that offer, and then agree to a soft peace with the French. I will ask only for a few colonies, to keep the Colonial Lobby quiet and provide coaling bases for Admiral Tirpitz's ships; say, Martinique in the Caribbean, Morocco or Tunisia in North Africa, and New Caledonia in the Pacific. There will be no indemnities and no

185

territorial claims on Metropolitan France. Do you agree with me that the French would accept such terms?"

"They would have to be insane not to," Moltke said. "May I ask Your Majesty why he intends to be so generous to our ancient enemy?"

"Because we want nothing from France; we need nothing from France," Wilhelm replied. "Germany's future lies in the East. When the treaty with Russia is finally signed, the Empire will add vast new territories for our people to settle, rich lands in Poland, the Ukraine, White Russia.

That is also why overseas colonies are unimportant: the valuable land is here, in Central Europe."

Moltke nodded, impressed. "And a soft peace with France will make it more difficult for her politicians to stir up hatred against Germany, so a future war becomes even less likely, and leaves Germany free to concentrate on developing our new lands in the East."

"Why is it that you can so easily understand what my ministers cannot?" the Kaiser exclaimed. "Perhaps I should make you Chancellor and send Holstein back to his estate."

"I have no desire for such responsibilities, Your Majesty," Moltke protested hastily, "and no ambition to enter politics. I am a simple soldier, and my only wish is to be permitted to continue to serve Your Majesty in that capacity."

"Come then, Field Marshal," said the Kaiser rising. "If you will not be my Chancellor, you must at least stand at my side on the palace balcony during the review, so that all the returning heroes from the East can see you."

Moltke rose from the couch, and together with his sovereign he strode off through the marble halls of the Royal Palace of the Hohenzollerns.

Chapter Nineteen: Bryn Mawr, August 16, 1915

The sun shined brightly as Ray Swing made his way across the grassy campus of Bryn Mawr College in suburban Philadelphia, site of the European Peace Conference. The exclusive women's college had been selected by President Wilson to host the Conference, he had been told, in order to escape the oppressive heat of Washington. Having experienced the nation's capital in the summer himself, Swing was grateful to be spared it.

He entered the Gothic Revival building where the diplomats were assembling. Since arriving at the Peace Conference a few days earlier, Swing had met a vast array of politicians, diplomats, soldiers and fellow reporters. Some he had forgotten almost before he left their company. Others had made lasting impressions on him, favorable or unfavorable. Out of this crowd of new faces and names, Swing thought the 31-year old Assistant Secretary of the Navy was the most memorable. Franklin Roosevelt was charming, witty and well informed about what was going on behind the scenes at the Conference. But beyond that, he had a certain electrifying air about him. Roosevelt had big ambitions and, Swing sensed, outstanding ability to match. His distant relative, Theodore, had been President of the United States (and one of the best ever, in Swing's opinion); with a little luck, he thought that this Roosevelt, from the Hyde Park branch of the family, had a chance to follow his famous fifth cousin.

In almost no time, he and Roosevelt picked up their conversation where they had left it the previous evening, swapping scurrilous rumors about members of the various diplomatic delegations. As he was relating a particularly juicy bit of gossip he had picked up from a code clerk, Swing saw across the room a familiar figure dressed in the U.S. Army officer's uniform of dark blue jacket and light blue trousers.

"Please excuse me, Franklin," Swing said, interrupting his story about the sexual forays of a Third Secretary from the French Embassy. "I just spotted an old friend I haven't spoken to in a while."

Roosevelt smiled amiably. "I'll let you go, Raymond, but only if you promise to explain exactly what Monsieur Levesque and the two young ladies did with that bathtub full of large-curd cottage cheese, the next time we meet."

Swing promised to finish the story at their next meeting, then made his way across the room until he stood behind the officer. He tapped him on the shoulder. "Hi, Joe. It's been a while," he said, extending his hand to Joseph Stilwell, who he now saw wore two gleaming bars of silver on each of his shoulder straps. "Congratulations on your promotion. I see someone upstairs finally had the sense to make you a captain. You probably should be a light colonel by now, if anybody wants my opinion."

Stilwell's lips curved up in a grin. "You know what they say," he replied as he shook Swing's hand, "the higher a monkey climbs up a pole, the more you see of his behind. Apparently, somebody at the War Department liked the work I did for them over in Berlin and…" he paused, looking a little embarrassed, and his voice dropped as he finished, "…Ambassador Gerard gave me an excellent evaluation and recommended the promotion."

"What?" asked Swing incredulously. "You mean the Ambastad…"

"Yeah," Stilwell interjected hurriedly. "Maybe I was a little unfair to him. But I think you have to take some of the credit, or the blame, as the case may be, old sport. That information you dug up on the chlorine gas program and the new torpedo really woke them up in

Washington. They finally realize how far behind the Krauts we are in weapons development."

"I'm glad to hear my information was worthwhile," said Swing. "Is that why you are here?"

"They wanted to have an expert on the German Army handy in case they needed one, and somebody seemed to think that I knew something about the subject," Stilwell said. "Let's get a cup of java and sit down for a real talk. I think we have a few minutes before the powwow resumes."

They were in a spacious, high-ceilinged lobby that served as the antechamber to the auditorium where the diplomats were negotiating. The lobby had a buffet set up along one wall containing coffee, tea, pastries, rolls and an assortment of cold cuts for the attendees. Stilwell and Swing each drew coffee from a silver urn, and then adjourned to a pair of vacant armchairs set on either side of a small table.

"The last time I saw you was back in January, before the Cracow Conference," Stilwell said. "You were there, so tell me about it. Kaiser Bill really squeezed the Russians, didn't he?"

"The Germans had a simple, but effective negotiating technique. Until the Czar's diplomats signed the treaty, their army kept advancing and all the land they occupied was added to German territory," Swing said. "You had to feel sorry for the Russians. They brought a former Premier, Count Kokovtsov, out of retirement to head their delegation. He made several very dignified and eloquent appeals to the Germans' sense of justice, which was like trying to get meat away from a shark by reasoning with it. After a week of these farcical negotiations, the Russians caved in and signed what the Germans put in front of them. They didn't really have a choice - Russia was incapable of continuing the war."

"It's no wonder they didn't want to sign. The terms of the treaty were brutal," Stilwell said. "Russian Poland

189

and the Ukraine split between Germany and Austria-Hungary; Bessarabia sliced off and handed to Romania; and Belorussia, Lithuania, Latvia, Estonia and Finland granted their 'independence'."

"Yes. Wasn't it odd that all these new 'independent' states picked members of the German nobility as their new rulers?" Swing asked. "And signed treaties which giving German Empire control over their armies, their foreign relations and, oh yes, their police."

"Who immediately arrested any nationalists who weren't quick enough to get out of their countries in time. The Germans aren't really trying very hard to pretend that the new 'nations' are anything but a sham to cover their expansion," Stilwell added. "They will all be annexed to Germany within a few months, is my guess."

"Except for Finland, Joe. Don't forget Finland," Swing reminded him. "But then, no German soldier ever set foot there. The Finns won their independence without help from anybody."

Stilwell nodded. "So what happens to Russia now?" he asked. "The Czar's abdication was too late to save the dynasty, and there's nobody really in charge there now."

"I think Russia is off the board as a Great Power for the next few years, at least," said Swing. "No matter who wins the civil war, the country has lost too much to recover anytime soon. Over in Cracow, I met an observer from the British Foreign Office, a real sharp cookie named Toynbee. He was a doing report for the Foreign Minister on the impact of the war on Russia. He estimated that under the Treaty of Cracow, Russian lost 25 percent of its population, 25 percent of its industry, 90 percent of its coalmines, and more than half of their railroad mileage. He had a lot more numbers, but the point is that Russia will be crippled for a long time to come."

"What worries me is how strong Germany is going to be when they finish digesting their new acquisitions and integrate them into the Empire," Stilwell said. "They're already plenty strong enough to suit me." His gaze shifted back to Swing. "But enough about that. Tell me what you've been up to. Did you interview that old fraud, Bryan? Did you meet Woodenhead Wilson?"

Swing brayed out a laugh so loud that a number of the occupants of the room ceased their conversations to momentarily stare at the source of the disturbance.

"Christ, Joe, don't repeat that to anybody else around here!" Swing finally said, after he had recovered the power of speech. "It'll be the end of your career. It's not a very appropriate nickname, anyway. Wilson's probably one of the most intelligent Presidents we've ever had." He stifled another laugh, then continued, "To answer your questions, I saw President Wilson at a news conference, but was not introduced to him. I did have a long interview with Secretary Bryan yesterday. He was very pleasant, like a kindly old uncle. I'm pretty well convinced that he really is motivated by a sincere desire for peace."

"Maybe," grunted Stilwell. "So why is it that whenever I see him, I think of the Wizard of Oz?"

Swing chuckled. "Come to think of it, he *does* have more than a passing resemblance to the pictures of the old humbug in the book. Do you suppose Baum based the Wizard on our distinguished Secretary of State?"

"Right, and the Cowardly Lion is supposed to be McKinley," Stilwell said, trying to match the absurdity of Swing's suggestion. "But getting back to matters at hand," he continued, "I'd like to hear your ideas on exactly why Kaiser Willy agreed to arbitrate, instead of just flattening the French and doing to them what he did to the Russians. I have a few thoughts on it myself, and I'm wondering how they compare to yours."

Swing rubbed his chin thoughtfully. "Well, I'm just speculating, but here's what I think. The Kaiser could win the war in the West whenever he wanted. The Germans could beat down the French the hard way, by a direct attack out of Alsace-Lorraine. It would be bloody, but with their big siege guns, their big numbers, and persistence, the Germans would eventually crack the Verdun-Toul fortress line, force a showdown with the French Army and crush it, if they didn't mind paying the price. But what would they do with France then? Put it under permanent military occupation? Annex it to Germany?"

Stilwell shook his head. "Not practical. How many men would they need to garrison the entire country? And how long before the uprisings started, before the *franc-tireurs* were assassinating Kraut officers and occupation officials?"

"Agreed," said Swing. "So, if the Germans didn't want to occupy France, why bother getting all those soldiers killed to take it? Once they knocked the Russians out, they knew the game was over, it was just a matter of raking in the pot. By letting Wilson and Bryan arbitrate, the Kaiser will look more reasonable, the French will be more likely to accept the treaty, and the war will be over that much sooner."

"After that, they can concentrate on absorbing all their land grabs in the East," Stilwell said. "I think that's about right. I figure this is not going to be a very long peace conference. The Germans will offer terms that the Frogs will be in no position to turn down, and you'll be filing your story on the signing ceremony before Labor Day."

The double doors of the main entrance swung open, and they saw two familiar figures silhouetted in the bright sunlight for a moment. They were closely followed by a gaggle of top-hatted diplomats, politicians, reporters and assorted hangers-on.

Stilwell rose. "I see that President Woodenhead and the Great and Powerful Oz have arrived, so I guess we both have to get back to work," he said.

Grinning, Swing stood up, and together, they followed the Presidential party into the auditorium.

CHICAGO DAILY NEWS
August 28, 1916

One Year After the Great European War:
Europe and the World
on the Anniversary of the Treaty of Bryn Mawr
by Senior Foreign Correspondent Ray Swing

...For France, the war was a mitigated disaster. The German terms were unexpectedly mild: the transfer to Germany of three French colonies; Martinique, New Caledonia and Morocco. There were no demands for indemnities, or for any concessions of territory from the French homeland by Germany. Above all, the Treaty of Bryn Mawr allowed France to escape a fate that had looked to be inevitable once Russia had been forced out of the war: a repeat of occupation by the hated *boches,* like the one that had followed the defeat of Napoleon III in 1871.

In almost every other respect however, the Great European War has proved to be a catastrophe for France.

France's colonial empire was gutted by the war. In addition to the three colonies transferred to Germany under the Treaty of Bryn Mawr, France's largest Asian possession was lopped off as well. Indochina was occupied by Japan in 1915, and subsequently annexed to the Japanese Empire.

The French Army was not very effective in combat against Germany. In particular, their artillery proved to be far too light for modern warfare. Imprudent military leadership was another element in the disaster. A succession of reckless attacks against strongly prepared German positions resulted in the loss of over a half-million men while gaining France nothing. The naval picture is even worse. The French fleet was practically obliterated in February 1915, at the Battle of Cape

Cepet. Although France is now engaged in a massive naval construction program, it will be years before she regains her status as a sea power.

The current government in Paris won its position as a result of the loss of the war. When the terms of the Treaty of Bryn Mawr were published, the French people, who had been told that they were winning the war, were outraged. Public anger was directed more at the government that had presided over the calamity than the Germans, and a coalition of Nationalists was swept into power in the elections of October of last year. The new Premier, George Clemenceau, emerged from retirement to take office on a platform of military and naval rearmament and a pledge to aggressively seek powerful new allies abroad.

But today, one year after the official end of the war, France remains in the diplomatic isolation ward. Her former ally, Russia, after undergoing dismemberment by Germany and Austria, and with civil war now raging in what remains, is in chaos. When, if ever, Russia will regain Great Power status is uncertain, but at the present time there is no power in Eastern or Central Europe available for France to cultivate as a potential ally and counterweight to Germany. Great Britain, under the Liberal government of Herbert Asquith, reacted to the war by backing further away from any commitment to France...

...By far the biggest change in the European scene since the war has been the vast growth in the German Empire. Added to Germany, either by direct appropriation or as thinly disguised puppet states, is a vast new territory comprising most of what had been Russian Poland, most of the Ukraine, as well as Belorussia, Latvia, Lithuania and Estonia. These new lands contain more than 50 million inhabitants and the greater part of what had been the best farmland in Russia. Included in this new territory are practically all the Russian coal mines and a least a quarter of all pre-war Russian industry...

The performance of the German Army in the war has gained it a well-deserved reputation as the best in the world. In contrast to the French, the Germans were prepared for the war in every way. The General Staff under Field Marshal von Moltke produced a miracle of improvisation in the decisive Battles of East Prussia, and repeatedly out-planned and out-fought the larger Russian Army. At the tactical level, German weapons, training and organization showed themselves to be at least the equal of any other in the world today. German artillery proved to be the decisive arm on the battlefield, repeatedly destroying Russian defensive positions, allowing the infantry to break through them again and again.

Germany had never been thought of as a sea power before 1914. That is no longer true. The Imperial German Navy, built to challenge the Royal Navy, proved its worth against the French. Thanks to new overseas bases in its newly acquired colonies, Germany is well positioned to project its naval power into all of the world's oceans.

Germany is now in a position of dominance over Europe unmatched by any nation since France at the height of the Napoleonic Empire. Her alliance with the only remaining Central European Great Power, Austria-Hungary, appears to be as strong as ever. Nowhere is there a rival alliance capable of challenging the German-led combination, and there is no sign of one on the horizon. Whether further plans for expansion are being made in Berlin today is unknown, but if they are not now, it is likely that at some time in the not very distant future, they will be.

...It is the opinion of this reporter that the government of the United States should begin to consider the danger posed by a greatly expanded, aggressive German Empire. It is not too early for our country to put aside its traditional policy of isolation and begin to seek alliances with other peaceful nations for the purpose of restraining Germany. The risk of being drawn into a war by such alliances is a real one, but that risk should weighed against the danger of being alone and friendless in the face of the greatest military power in history.

The End

Afterword One:
Counterfactually Speaking:
Of the Great War, alternate history and related matters

Alternate history, disguised under the somewhat more respectable name of "counterfactual history", has recently enjoyed considerable interest in academic circles. Using a counterfactual, the impact of an historical event can be measured by imagining what would happen if it had occurred differently, and then examining the ways in which subsequent events would have been altered. I believe that the triggering event selected should meet two essential criteria. First, the event should be pivotal to subsequent history. Second, there must be a realistic chance that the event could have actually happened in the "counterfactual" way.

As the history of the Great War (later called the First World War) may not be familiar to some readers, particularly in America, they may find a brief summary of the war's main events useful for comparison with the war depicted herein.

The war in the West commences with the German invasion of Belgium on August 3, 1914. Great Britain, invoking its obligations under the Treaty of London, declares war on Germany on August 4. The French counter the German invasion with Plan XVII, launching most of their armies into offensives in Alsace and Lorraine. These attacks accomplish nothing, and cost France a quarter-million men.

The overextended German right wing is defeated at the Battle of the Marne on September 5, and the war in the West soon settles into a deadlock, with lines of trenches stretching across northern France from the

English Channel to the Swiss border. Great Britain, which initially contributes only a small professional army of fewer than 250,000 men, now begins to raise a mass army taken from all parts of the Empire. By 1918, the British Army will number more than 4 million men.

The day Great Britain enters the war, the Royal Navy imposes a blockade on Germany. The blockade continues until after the end of the war, and by 1918 is causing serious food shortages in Germany. The German main battle fleet remains penned up in its ports for most of the war, coming out to offer battle only once, in 1916. The resulting Battle of Jutland is inconclusive, but the blockade remains in place and the German High Seas Fleet stays in port for the rest of the war.

To counter the British blockade, Germany employs a relatively new weapon: the submarine. The Kaiser declares the waters around the British Isles to be a war zone, and his submarines begin to sink any ship that enters it, including neutral vessels. By 1917, submarines have sunk several passenger liners carrying Americans, and dozens of American ships. Unrestricted submarine warfare fails to starve out Great Britain, and proves to be the major reason that the United States joins the war against Germany, in 1917.

In the East, the Russians take a desperate gamble, sending the only half-ready Russian First and Second Armies to invade East Prussia at the beginning of August. Although outnumbered 4 to 1, the German Eighth Army smashes and nearly destroys the Russian Second Army at the Battle of Tannenburg, then defeats the Russian First Army at the Battle of the Masurian Lakes, so that by the end of August, the initial Russian offensive has been thrown back with heavy losses. The Russians are more successful on the southern half of the front against Germany's ally, defeating the Austro-Hungarian armies in early battles, and overrunning a large swathe of Austrian territory.

While stalemate continues in the West until 1918, in the East, German armies under Generals Hindenburg and Ludendorff, heroes of the Battle of Tannenburg, defeat the Russians repeatedly. By 1917, the economy of Russia, strained to the limits to supply munitions for the army, collapses, and the morale of the army crumbles. The Czar is overthrown in March, replaced by a Provisional Government which continues to prosecute the war. But by now, most of the soldiers are sick of the war, and refuse to fight. In November, the Provisional Government is overthrown in turn by the Bolsheviks led by Lenin, who has been sent into Russia by the Germans in the hopes that he will sow revolution there. In March 1918, the Bolshevik government is forced to sign the Treaty of Brest-Litovsk, surrendering huge areas of Russia to the German Empire. The Russian Civil War continues until 1922, ending with a Bolshevik victory.

In France, both sides attempt to break the trench deadlock with head-on attacks, which are repeatedly and bloodily defeated. At the Somme in 1916, the British lose 60,000 men on the first day, and over 600,000 in the 4 1/2 month long battle to win 6 miles of shell-pocked dirt. The same year, at Verdun, the French and Germans fight for nine months and suffer nearly a million casualties altogether. There is, by the end, no significant change in the trench lines.

By 1917, the contestants are beginning to run out of men. In 1918, Ludendorff, who by now is the virtual dictator of Germany, makes a final effort to win the war by bringing 50 divisions to France from the now quiet Eastern Front. With this additional manpower and new weapons and tactics, he hopes to shatter the Allied line and destroy their armies before the United States can bring in enough new men to tip the balance of the war against Germany. The Ludendorff Offensives of 1918 do break through at several points, but the Allies simply retreat, shorten their defensive lines and, with American troops patching some of the holes, eventually stop the

German advance without being annihilated. After the failure of the Ludendorff Offensives and the heavy losses the attackers sustain, the German Army is seriously weakened. A series of Allied offensives, beefed up by the presence of a fresh American Army (the United States will send 4.7 million men to France before the war's end) recaptures all the territory lost in the Ludendorff Offensives. By November, the German Army is near collapse. So too is the German Empire's economy, as a result of the blockade. Bad news from the front, starvation and war weariness lead to revolution in the streets. The Kaiser is forced to abdicate, and a new civilian government asks for an armistice.

The Austro-Hungarian Empire, considered by many to be on the verge of disintegration even before 1914, surprises many observers by surviving four years of total war. However, it does so only by becoming a virtual German dependency. In 1918, no longer propped up by Germany, the Empire falls to pieces. The Austrian Army stops fighting when the Italians attack in October 1918 at Vittorio Veneto. (Italy had been bribed to join the Entente in 1915, with promises that she would be rewarded with the Austrian Trentino and Fiume after the war.) The Austro-Hungarian Empire now disappears from the map of Europe, to be replaced by the new independent republics of Czechoslovakia, Poland, Yugoslavia, Austria and Hungary.

Gray Tide in the East branches off from the above history in Chapter One, when General Helmuth von Moltke, Chief of the Imperial General Staff of Germany commits an act of near *lese-majesty*, prompting the Kaiser to cancel the invasion of Belgium. Up to that point, the story follows actual events. Wilhelm did order the invasion stopped on August 1, using the note from Ambassador Lichnowski described in the text as the reason. The conversation between the Kaiser and his general is based on Moltke's memoirs, and cited in Barbara Tuchman's incomparable account of the opening days of the war, *The Guns of August* (New York, 1962), p. 79. (If you have the slightest interest in the Great War and have not read this book, I urge you to do so.) Wilhelm's hasty decision is the triggering event this story explores.

The thesis of this book is that if the Kaiser had not reversed his decision to abandon the invasion of Belgium, the Triple Alliance would have won the war. My reasoning is as follows: without the invasion of Belgium to provide a *casus belli*, Great Britain would not have entered the war in 1914. The Asquith Government was lukewarm towards France at best, and the Liberal majority in Parliament was dead set against being drawn into the Continental war. Evidence in support of this proposition comes from the diaries and memoirs of Prime Minister Asquith, Sir Edward Grey, Ambassador Paul Cambon and others, as cited in *The Guns of August*, especially p.77-81 (Grey's "offer" to Lichnowski), and p.94-97 (regarding the position of His Majesty's Government, the country's unwillingness to enter the war and Ambassador Cambon's protestations to Grey.)

It follows that if Great Britain does not enter the war, the Royal Navy has no occasion to impose the blockade that eventually proved to be so ruinous to the German economy. It is unlikely that the German blockade of France as described in *Gray Tide* would have been sufficient to provide a *casus belli*. Great Britain had for centuries gone to great lengths to establish the naval blockade as a legitimate method of warfare under international law, because the Royal Navy was the principal instrument of British power. It was largely for this reason that the British accepted the Union blockade of the Confederacy during the American Civil War, even when the resulting loss of cotton imports threatened the English economy. For these reasons, there is little likelihood that the Asquith Government

201

would have abandoned the principle of the blockade to intervene on behalf of France.

In the absence of the British blockade, Germany would have had no reason to employ unrestricted submarine warfare against Britain or anyone else. Under these circumstances, it is nearly certain that the United States would not have entered the war. (Woodrow Wilson won re-election in 1916 running on the slogan, "He kept us out of war." This was *after* the sinking of the *Lusitania* in 1915 by U-20, which had resulted in the drowning of nearly 1200 people, including 128 Americans, in addition to many other sinkings of American vessels by U-boats. Most Americans did not want any part of this war.)

What is left is the Triple Alliance consisting Germany, Austria-Hungary and Italy (see *note*) against the Dual Entente of Russia and France.

Given the foregoing, I conclude that the French–Russian coalition, without the aid of the British Empire, would have been defeated by the Triple Alliance. There is some quantitative support for this conclusion in Chapter 5 of Paul Kennedy's *The Rise and Fall of the Great Powers* (New York, 1987). Of special note is table 22 on p.258 where Kennedy calculates the total "industrial potential" of Germany and Austria-Hungary at 178.4 compared with that of the Franco-Russian combination at only 133.9. This calculation does not even take into account the addition of Italy which, as noted above, I believe would have joined the other members of the Triple Alliance, if Great Britain had stayed out of the war. Nor does it include the damage to the economy of France caused by the German blockade.

Note*: Italy declined to enter the war in 1914 alongside its partners in the Triple Alliance, claiming that their treaty obligations were strictly "defensive", that Austria's dealings with Serbia were "offensive", and that Italy was therefore excused from its treaty commitment. However, Italy's reluctance was more* *likely caused by Great Britain's entry into the war. This is another consequence of the German invasion of Belgium. For relevant diplomatic correspondence, see: http://www.firstworldwar.com/ source/italianneutrality.htm*

By contrast, a table on page 271 of *Rise and Fall* shows the overwhelming industrial might of the combination that eventually won the war. The total industrial potential of the U.S.-British-French alliance that prevailed in 1918 was 472.6, compared to the German-Austrian total of only 178.4. These numbers support Kennedy's thesis that, over the course of a long war, the nation or coalition with the greatest industrial resources will prevail, all other things being roughly equal (this caveat leaves room for exceptions like the Vietnam War and the American Revolution).

An almost equally important question is whether it was even possible for the Germans to have turned the entire weight of their attack to the East at the last minute without causing the chaos that Moltke feared. The answer to this depends on how much credence one puts in the post-war claims of General Herman von Staab, the Director of the Division of Military Railways. It should be remembered the efficiency of the German Railway Division of the General Staff rose to the level of legend after the role it played in organizing the German railroads in victorious wars against Denmark, Austria and France in the half-century preceding World War One. I rely for the outcome here on the book by Staab after the war. It was written to refute Moltke's post-war statement that the transfer of the 750,000 men of the right wing from the Western Front to the East would have been impossible. In *Aufmarsch nach zwei Fronten: auf Grund der Operationspläne von 1870-1914 (March on Two Fronts: on the Basis of the Operational Plans of 1870-1914)* General von Staab definitively states that German deployment could have been changed from

West to East even as late as the first week of August 1914.

A comparatively minor, but still interesting issue, is whether the Chief of the General Staff would have backed down under these circumstances, or instead would have offered the Kaiser his resignation. When considering this, it is worth noting that Moltke was uncomfortable with the vast responsibilities that his position entailed. At a critical moment during the Battle of the Marne, with the outcome of the war possibly riding in the balance, he delegated a critical decision to a subordinate, a lowly Colonel (the self-same Col. Hentch in Chapter 1) (*The Guns of August*, p. 431). Given that he had reservations about the wisdom of the Schlieffen Plan in the first place, it is not so difficult to believe that Moltke would have been secretly grateful to be relieved of the burden by orders from above.

The rationale for the outcome of the Battles of East Prussia herein should not be very difficult to understand. What the outnumbered German 8th Army did at the Battle of Tannenburg and the First Battle of the Masurian Lakes could have been done in spades with the addition of 750,000 men transferred from the Western Front.

The main source for my description of the rout of the XV Corps in Chapter 4 is a paper written at the Leavenworth General Staff School in 1933 by Major Edgemont F. Koenig, entitled "A Critical Analysis of the Battle of Morhange-Sarreborg," which can be found at:

The Combined Arms Research Library Digital Library

http://cgsc.contentdm.oclc.org/cdm/singleitem/colle ction/p4013coll14/id/995/rec/1

In the Great War, it took the French High Command more than a year to adjust to the gigantic siege operation of the Western Front. General Joseph Joffre, the French Commander-in-Chief, persisted in employing the same near-suicidal tactics in 1915 that had already failed so spectacularly in 1914, launching offensives in Champagne and Artois that resulted in enormous French losses without gaining a single positive result. Indeed, Joffre never absorbed the lessons about the defensive power of barbed wire, machine guns and rapid-firing modern artillery taught by the early battles of the war. As a result, he was promoted to Field Marshal in 1916 and kicked upstairs to remove his dead weight.

Thus in *Gray Tide*, the French continue to apply their *offensive à outrance* tactics in their spring offensive in the mountains, with the same grisly results as before. An excellent source for the development of French tactics before the war as discussed in Chapters 4 and 15 is "No Other Law: The French Army and the Doctrine of Offensive" by Charles W. Saunders, Jr., the Rand Corporation, Santa Monica, CA. 1987 at:

http://www.rand.org/content/dam/rand/pubs/papers/2005/P7331.pdf.

The Japanese takeover of Indochina in Chapter 13 is based in part on what actually happened to the German Pacific colonies in the Great War, combined with occurred in Indochina in the Second World War. In 1914, Japan took advantage of Germany's difficulties to snap up several German colonies in the Pacific, including the Marshall Islands, the Caroline Islands and the Marianas Islands, as well as the German leasehold in China at Kiautschou, while the Germans were busy elsewhere and their fleet was blockaded by the Royal Navy. In World War II, the Japanese invaded and seized Indochina in September 1940, after the French had been defeated by Hitler, and the weak Vichy government was helpless to do anything to stop them. Given that historical record, it is not difficult to imagine Japan taking advantage of French difficulties, as portrayed here.

In this alternate, Germany carves a huge new empire out of what had been Russia. This actually

205

happened in 1918; however, Germany was forced to disgorge all of this real estate at the Versailles Peace Conference after being defeated in the West. In 1918, the occupying Germans organized the three Baltic States of Latvia, Lithuania and Estonia into a short-lived puppet state known as the Baltic State Duchy, with Kaiser Wilhelm II as the first Duke. (See Thomas, N. and Bujeiro, R. *The German Army in World War I, 1917-1918*, Vol. 3, Oxford (U.K.), 2004.) Further evidence of German intentions in Eastern Europe after the defeat of Russia is the *Ober Ost*, political units in Western Russia created in 1918, with an eye towards settling German soldiers there after the war, along with the more immediate goal of shipping all the food surplus of the region to Germany to support the war effort. (*See* Gettman, E. *The Baltic Region During World War One*, 2002, http://depts.washington.edu/baltic/papers/worldwar1.htm)

The domination of the Mediterranean by the Triple Alliance described in the story logically follows from Great Britain's neutrality. The entire French Navy was only marginally superior to either the Italian or Austro-Hungarian Navy in 1914. The two combined, along with the much more powerful German High Seas Fleet, could have easily controlled the Mediterranean.

The account of the Galician offensive in Chapter 17 is based in part on the successful German-Austrian Gorlice-Tarnow Offensive of May 1915, but with more men and a much larger artillery preparation. Although the Russians were routed, they eventually recovered, re-established a defensive line and continued to fight for two more years. In the story, the force of the blow is even more devastating, and the Russian lines have been thinned by the removal of units which had been sent North in attempt to stem the gray tide along the Baltic.

Lieutenant Colonel Max Hoffman (1869-1927) began the war as the deputy chief of staff of the Eighth Army. He devised the plan that resulted in the destruction of the Russian Second Army at the Battle of Tannenburg for which Hindenburg and Ludendorff received most of the credit, and which launched the latter two men to the heights of fame. By the end of the war, Hoffman, by then a general, was in effective command of all the German and Austrian armies on the Eastern Front. His offensive in 1917 proved to be the final Russian defeat of the war, causing the overthrow of the Provisional Government, knocking Russia out of the war and forcing the Bolshevik Government to sign the humiliating Treaty of Brest-Litovsk.

Sub-Lieutenant Stephen King-Hall (1893-1966), served in the Royal Navy from 1914 to 1929, rising to the rank of Commander. He later became a member of the Royal Institute of International Affairs, and served as a Member of Parliament during the Second World War. He also wrote several plays, and was created a Baron in 1966. His account of his wartime experiences on the light cruiser HMS *Southampton*, entitled *North Sea Diary 1914-1918*, is available in excepted form at: *WWI Resource   Centre* (http://www.vlib.us/wwi/resources/northseadiary.html)

Commodore Reginald Tyrwhitt (later Admiral of the Fleet Sir Reginald Yorke Tyrwhitt, 1st Baronet, GCB, DSO) (1870-1951), commanded all destroyer flotillas of the Home Fleet at the beginning of the war, flying his flag in the light cruiser, HMS *Amethyst*. His leadership was highly regarded, and his Harwich Force participated in the Battle of Heligoland Bight, the Cuxhaven Raid in 1914, and the Battle of Dogger Bank in 1915. Tyrwhitt was created a Baronet in 1919, and promoted to Admiral of the Fleet in 1934 after a long, distinguished career. (Biographical material courtesy of the   Dreadnought   Project, http://dreadnoughtproject.org/tfs/index.php /Reginald_Yorke_Tyrwhitt,_First_Baronet)

Raymond Gram Swing (1887-1968) was a journalist and head of the *Chicago Daily News* Berlin bureau in

1914. As a war correspondent he covered the 1915 Gallipoli campaign from the Turkish side and many other war stories. He later became a pioneer in radio journalism. His coverage of the 1932 American presidential election brought him an offer from CBS to set up a radio news network in Europe. He turned down this offer, and the position was given to Edward R. Murrow. He instead signed in 1936 with the Mutual Radio Network, covering Europe, and went on to a long and distinguished career in broadcasting with ABC, BBC and the Voice of America. (Biographical material from Wikipedia and the *New York Times* obituary December 24, 1968.)

On one minor matter, I must confess to cheating a bit. Joseph Stilwell (1883-1946), who appears several times in the story as the military attaché to the Embassy in Berlin, never served in Germany. (He did serve as a military attaché in China in 1935-37, however, and organized a spy network there as part of his duties.) He was a brilliant combat soldier, who eventually rose to the rank of 4-star General as the commanding officer of the China-India-Burma Theatre in World War 2. My excuse for putting him where he certainly never was is that I find him to be a compelling historical figure, and my favorite American soldier. I do not believe that his presence in Berlin in 1914 would have had any significant effect on the major historical events as set forth in this book. For a portrait of this American original combined with a lucid account of the failure of America's China policy, I heartily recommend Barbara Tuchman's *Stilwell and the American Experience in China* (New York, 1970).

The remarkable story of Albert Dawson (1885-1967), the long forgotten pioneer documentary filmmaker is told by Ron van Doppern in "Shooting the Great War: Albert Dawson and the American Correspondent Film Company, 1914-1918," *Film History* , vol. 4, No. 2, University of Indiana Press, 1990.

(For those curious as to the fate of Dawson's film, but not curious enough to track down the van Doppern article, I will summarize here. Dawson's production company, the American Correspondent Film Company, had been kept afloat by German government money. Apparently, the film was about to be released in America just when Berlin pulled the plug on the ACFC and the company promptly folded. The film trade journal, *Moving Picture World*, reviewed *Battle and Fall of Przemysl* in the Current Productions section of the August 14, 1915 issue. *See*: (https://play.google.com/books/reader?id=eUs_ AAAAYAAJ&printsec=frontcover&output =reader&authuser   =0&hl=en&pg=GBS.PA1174). Sadly, the film was never shown in this country, and Dawson's career in filmmaking ended in 1918. He died in 1965 in obscurity, his film lost in the mists of time.

Adolf Hitler (1889-1945) was a German war hero, winning the Iron Cross First and Second Class on the Western Front. He was wounded twice in combat, and gassed in 1918. He became prominent in German politics in the 1920s and 30s as the leader of the National Socialist Workers Party.

The brief conversation in Chapter Nineteen concerning the possible resemblance of William Jennings Bryan and William McKinley to characters in the fantasy *The Wizard of Oz* by L. Frank Baum is a direct reference to the interpretation of that book by Henry Littlefield, a high school teacher, which has gained wide currency since it was first propounded in 1964. Littlefield's interpretation, based on the assumption that Baum was a pro-silver Bryan Democrat, for which Littlefield had not the slightest evidence, was that Baum's novel was actually an allegory of the Gold and Silver Election of 1896. In fact, research by Baum biographers shows that he was probably a Republican. This completely explodes Littlefield's theory, and he was forced to admit that "there is no basis in fact to consider

Baum a supporter of turn-of-the-century Populist ideology." Yet this bogus allegory theory continues to be cited in both popular works and scholarly journals for some reason. See *The Historian's Wizard of Oz*, Ranjit S. Dighe, ed., (Westport, Conn., 2002), Chapter One.

The description of the Berlin Guildhall Rathskeller in Chapter 10, including the translation of the poem inscribed on the central column, comes from *Berlin Under the New Empire*, Volume 2, by Henry Vizetelly (London, 1879).

For general background on the origins of the war, I am indebted to Laurence Lafore's excellent *The Long Fuse* (Philadelphia and New York, 1965).

Below are some of the Internet resources without which this book would not have been possible:

For naval matters, especially for facts about the French Navy, *Navypedia*: (http://www.navypedia.org/ships/france.htm); for facts and figures on warships of all the participants, the *Dreadnought Project*, a website devoted to all things dreadnought:

(http://www.dreadnoughtproject.org) and *WWI, the War At Sea* (http://www.gwpda.org/naval/n0000000.htm), an essential source for naval information on all the major powers, with the names, classes, and details of individual ships, including HMS *Southampton*.

Much more about the Lohner B.VI and other aircraft of the Austro-Hungarian Royal and Imperial Aviation Corps can be found at *Military Factory* (http://www.militaryfactory.com/aircraft/ww1-austria-hungary-military-aircraft.asp)

For all kinds of background material and leads to other sources, *The First World War.com* (http://www.firstworldwar.com) was invaluable.

Afterword Two
The War That Was and the War That Was Not:
World War One and the Great European War

Gray Tide in the East is a thought experiment in counter-factual history. Where in the preceding essay I described the details of the experiment, I will here discuss some of the consequences of World War One (WWI) of history versus those of the Great European War (GEW) of this book.

To begin, after the GEW, there would have almost certainly been no Nazi Party to take power in Germany, thus Adolf Hitler would not have become the dictator who would bring about the Second World War almost single-handedly.

In August 1914, Kaiser Wilhelm enjoyed the overwhelming popularity and support of the citizens of the Empire. The Kaiser's power in the state was unchallenged. It was almost unthinkable that he would be forced to abdicate his throne just four years later, after defeat on the battlefield, famine at home and revolution in the streets. It was this defeat, after four terrible years of war, combined with the effects of the Depression which created the conditions that brought the National Socialist Party to power in 1932. One of Hitler's most powerful appeals to voters was the promise that he would avenge the humiliating defeat of 1918. Obviously, if there had been no defeat in 1918, this would not have been a very effective campaign pledge.

In any case, it is almost impossible to imagine a radical Right political party like the Nazis being successful in a German Empire basking in a glorious victory of a war led by the popular Hohenzollern

Dynasty. Even if something like the Nazi Party did form in post-war Germany (which would be very unlikely), the Kaiser's government would not have tolerated their violent ideas or their street-fighter tactics, and would have very quickly suppressed the movement and jailed its leaders.

The GEW would have also had a profound effect on the career of the British statesman who, along with Hitler, Stalin and Franklin Delano Roosevelt was one of the most important political figures of the 20th Century: Winston Churchill. In August, 1914, Churchill was 39 years old, and the coming man in the Liberal Party. He had already served in cabinet posts under the Asquith Government as President of the Board of Trade and Home Secretary before taking over the Admiralty in 1911, and seemed but a short step from becoming Prime Minister before his 45th birthday. But the war blighted his political career for many years. He was blamed (wrongly) for the disastrous Gallipoli campaign, which was a poorly designed and mismanaged attempt to invade Turkey and capture its capital, and became an 8 month bloodbath (April 1915- January 1916) ending in the humiliating defeat of the British forces by the Turks. (Churchill had wanted to use naval forces only to force the Dardanelles, bring Istanbul under the guns of British battleships, and force the Ottomans to make peace. If successful, this would also have opened up a supply route between Russia and its Entente partners, and very possibly changed the course of the war on the Eastern Front.) As a result of the Gallipoli catastrophe, Churchill was forced out of the Cabinet, and his rise to power delayed many years. In the GEW, where the British Empire remains on the sidelines, there would be no Gallipoli, and no reason to think that Churchill's political career would be harmed by the war. In the normal course of events, it is likely that he would have followed Asquith as the PM. (Churchill biographical material courtesy of The Winston Churchill Centre, http://www.winstonchurchill.org/, and William Manchester's incomparable biography *The Last Lion*, vol. 1, Boston, 1983).

For Great Britain, the result of the GEW as depicted in this book would have been in many ways much better than that of WWI. The negative is foreshadowed in Chapters 2, 7 and 18. After the GEW, Germany would have dominated the Continent militarily and economically. She would have posed a potential challenge to the British Empire after the war with the expansion of her own Imperial holdings and the newly enhanced status of the High Seas Fleet, after a victorious campaign in which she won every sea battle and successfully imposed a blockade on France, in true Royal Navy style.

On the other side of the coin... in WWI, the British Empire ended up on the winning side, but at the cost of over one million men killed and more than 2 million wounded. Great Britain alone suffered 886,000 dead (over 2% of the population) and 1.6 million wounded. A large portion of an entire generation of men who would have otherwise become the leaders of the Empire in the decades after the war was sacrificed in the mud of northern France.

WWI had a drastic effect on Great Britain as the world's banker and the City of London as its financial center, roles they had filled for a hundred years. In August 1914, the Bank of England announced that it was suspending gold payments against pounds sterling, in other words, abandoning the gold standard. The result was that the center of international finance shifted to Wall Street in the United States, never to return. As WWI dragged on and the combatant countries needed to borrow more money, the United States, not Great Britain, became the recipient of this immense (and immensely profitable) business. (See John Brooks' excellent study of Wall Street in the 1920s and '30s, *Once in Golconda,* New York, 1969, p. 3-5.)

Although Great Britain's GDP (Gross Domestic Product) increased slightly during the war, this was achieved in part by expending 15% of the nation's pre-war wealth, by massive borrowing and by production of huge quantities of munitions, whose value after the war was negligible. Moreover, the increase did little for British consumers, since by 1917 the government was absorbing 40% of the GDP compared with only 8% in 1913. Finally, the post WWI British economy was further crippled by the indirect costs of the war such as pensions for widows and soldiers crippled in the war, the loss of skilled labor, and so on. (War expenditure figures here and below are from *Rise and Fall of the Great Powers*, p. 274 and "Societies at War: Britain and France 1914-1918," by Dr. Paul Mulvey, London, 2011:

http://www.academia.edu/1093598/Societies_at_war_Britain_and_France_on_the_Home_Front_1914-18_lecture_ and *The Economics of World War One: a Comparative Quantitative Analysis* by Stephen Broadberry and Mark Harrison, University of Warwick, 2005.)

The ties that bound the Empire together were weakened by the four years of WWI. Australia, New Zealand and Canada, who had eagerly sent their young men to aid the mother country in 1914, after the war came to resent what they saw as the reckless sacrifice of their young men by British generals at battles like Vimy Ridge in France and in the Gallipoli Campaign. (For an understanding of why the Australians felt this way, see the 1981 film *Gallipoli*, directed by Peter Weir and starring Mel Gibson.) Canada lost almost 1% of its population, Australia 1.3% and New Zealand 1.6% fighting a war in which they had no direct stake. They would answer the call again in 1939, but not so eagerly and not as colonies. As a result of the Great War, the Balfour Declaration at the Imperial Conference of 1926 granted independence to all three countries (the Declaration was ratified in Australia and New Zealand in

214

1942 and 1947 respectively). Thus, the Empire did not last very many years after victory in 1918. There is no reason to suppose that a GEW in which Great Britain was neutral would have had any negative effect on the Empire, and no reason to think it would have endured for many more years.

If the result of the GEW depicted herein was a mitigated disaster for France, victory in 1918 in WWI was a complete catastrophe, with a worse outcome for France in almost every measurable way.

The French Army, in four years of trench warfare, sustained 1,679,000(!) dead, amounting to more than 4% of the country's population, and suffered a proportionate number of wounded: more than four million. This was out of a total population of less than 40 million. (All casualty figures are from *Wikipedia*:

http://en.wikipedia.org/wiki/World_War_I_casualti es.)

By contrast, in the GEW, I estimate French casualties at around 500,000 after approximately one year of war.

As for the monetary costs of WWI, where Great Britain expended 15% of her pre-war national wealth, France mortgaged her future by spending nearly 55% of her accumulated national wealth for essentially no return. The attempt to ameliorate some of these costs by imposing reparations on Germany as part of the peace settlement ended in failure, and was a public relations disaster for France. If this was victory, it was of a kind which was indistinguishable from defeat. It was this "victory" which planted the seeds of defeat in 1940, when the demoralized French Army was defeated by the Wehrmacht in just six weeks.

The preceding only goes to show that defeat in a short war can be less costly than victory in a long one. The GEW would have been better for all the participants than WWI actually was (with the possible exception of

215

Russia), if only because one year of war is better than four.

Even Russia, the big loser in the GEW, would not have suffered nearly as much as she did in WWI, at least her people would not have. Russia lost approximately 3½ million dead as a result of WWI, including a million civilians who died of disease or famine as a direct consequence of the war. These numbers would of course, have been far lower in the GEW, for reasons already stated.

Mention of Russia brings up the question of whether the Bolsheviks would have succeeded in establishing the world's first Communist government after the GEW. I am inclined to think that they would not. For one thing, Germany actually helped start the Bolshevik Revolution in 1917, by sending Lenin into Russia on a sealed train in the hope that he would be able to disrupt the Provisional Government, which was still bent on prosecuting the war. In the GEW, this would certainly not have occurred.

Then, even if the Bolsheviks had somehow managed to seize power in Russia, or even looked as if they were about to do so, it is quite likely that Germany would have made certain they would not have remained in power very long. The Kaiser would never have tolerated a Marxist revolutionary government on his border. At home, the German equivalents of the Bolsheviks were outlawed, and their leaders either in prison, in hiding or in exile. It is difficult to say what kind of government would finally have emerged in Russia after the GEW, but if it were not friendly to Germany, it would at least have been one that Germany could tolerate.

Eventually however, I would expect Russia to emerge after the GEW, revolution and civil war as a Great Power again, whether it took ten, fifteen or even twenty years to recover. The borders of Russia in 2013 are very similar to where they would have been left by

216

Germany after the Treaty of Cracow at the end of the GEW, and no one disputes Russia's Great Power status today. It is still a very big country, with a large population and immense natural resources.

For the United States, WWI was the beginning of her rise to world power. The United States was the only major participant in WWI (excluding Japan's very limited involvement) to enjoy a net benefit from the conflict. The U.S. economy boomed during WWI, supplying food, fuel and other raw materials to the Entente Powers, and was a major source of munitions. Even more profitable for the U.S. was its role as the banker to the Triple Entente, floating billions of dollars in war loans to the combatants. After the war, the U.S. was in an even stronger position in the commercial world, as the economies of all her potential rivals (except Japan) had been badly strained or crippled by WWI as set forth above. The American rise to a position of global military-political dominance by 1945 began with the industrial boom resulting from WWI. The relatively short GEW would certainly not have had any such effect. It would be more likely that the newly enlarged German Empire would rise to the top of the manufacturing world, once it had assimilated its new acquisitions. Would this eventually have led to a war between these two Powers? If Germany attempted to throw its weight around by trying to exclude American products from European markets, such an outcome is not unlikely.

One of the less obvious ways in which American history would have been altered by the events described in *Gray Tide*, is the effect of the Kaiser's decision canceling the invasion of Belgium on Prohibition. The 18th Amendment to the Constitution, outlawing the sale and production of alcoholic beverages, gained approval as a wartime measure. Proponents of the Prohibition claimed that it would make more grain available for the war effort, and would also result in more efficient workers, with fewer accidents and fewer days lost to drunkenness. Of course, the war ended before the Amendment had been ratified by the States in 1919, but it was too late to un-burn the bridge by then. Without Prohibition, the rise of the underworld empires built by Al Capone and his colleagues would not have been possible. Before Prohibition, it is true that there were crime gangs and families, but these were all local, or at most regional, in scope. Profits from the production, transportation and sale of alcohol (primarily beer) gave organized crime its start as a national phenomenon, one which we still have with us today.

One important subject which is touched on only briefly and tangentially in *Gray Tide* is the Ottoman Empire. WWI had a profound effect on the empire that later became the Republic of Turkey. By 1914, it was obvious to practically all observers that the crumbling Ottoman Empire (often referred to as "The Sick Man of Europe") was on its last legs. Defeated in 1912 in the First Balkan War by a coalition of Serbia, Bulgaria, Greece and Montenegro, the Turkish Empire had lost most of its European territories, and whatever remained of its Great Power status. It seemed only a matter of time until its final collapse. In 1914, the Ottomans joined the Central Powers, hoping to recoup some of their lost territory.

After the war, the Ottoman Empire was, like Austria-Hungary, dismantled, under the terms of the Treaty of Sèvres (1920). A slew of new nations were created out of what had been imperial provinces: Syria, Lebanon, Thrace Armenia, Palestine. All of these new entities were made League of Nations "mandates" and turned over to Great Britain and France for administration. Anatolia, the Turkish homeland, was carved up into "zones of influence" controlled by various members of the victorious coalition, including Greece, France, Great Britain and Italy. The end of the Ottoman Empire also meant the beginning of Arab sovereignty in the Middle East, with the creation of first modern independent Arab state, the Kingdom of Hejaz (Saudi Arabia).

In the GEW, the Ottomans end up on the winning team, and rather than collapsing, the Empire would presumably have continued to totter along (although for how many more years is far from clear). Depending on how long the Ottoman Empire persisted, the advent of Arab nationhood could have been set back many years. Before the war, the Ottomans had been assiduously courted by Germany, which was attempting to extend its influence into the Mediterranean region with major economic investments, such as the Berlin to Baghdad Railway. It is possible that the rulers of the Empire would have found a way to revitalize itself and modernize its economy, as a result of German and other foreign investment, allowing it to remain viable well into the 20th Century. If this had happened, it is likely that the Arab nations which we know today might never have come into existence at all.

Another subject related to the Ottoman Empire which the book does not touch upon, is the Armenian Genocide, which began in April, 1915. By the end of the war in 1918, the Turks had killed, according to best estimates, 1.5 million Armenians (estimated deaths vary from 600,000 to more than 2 million. See: http://books.google.com/books?id=nnUR4hSTb8gC &pg=PA44 Auron, Yair. New Brunswick, 2000).

This was the first attempt by a modern state to exterminate an entire people, and this effort by the Ottoman Turks to destroy the Armenians became a model and inspiration for others to follow, most notably the Nazis. Unfortunately, this important story fell outside the scope of the main story, and coverage of it would have required radical changes in the structure of the book.

I think it likely that the alliance between Germany and Austria-Hungary would have broken up after the

GEW during the 1920s... Without the fear of a mutual enemy (Russia) to keep Austria-Hungary attached to Germany, friction over issues such as the spoils of the war (Germany would, as the dominant partner, undoubtedly keep all the best pieces of Russia for herself, throwing the scraps and leavings to Austria), the treatment of minorities in the Dual Monarchy (Austrian policy was beginning to favor the ruling German minority sharing power with various ethnic groups within the Empire; the German Empire believed that everyone should be assimilated and that all former ethnic ties should be forgotten), and so on. Therefore, it is certainly possible that not very many years after the end of the GEW, Austria-Hungary might have become the Eastern ally for which France was searching, especially since the two nations had no direct cause for enmity, and both were bordered by the same large and dangerous Power.

With regard to the future of the Mediterranean after the GEW, my own views are expressed by Commodore Tyrwhitt in Chapter 7. Germany would not have been able to keep the troika of Austria-Hungary, Italy and Turkey pulling in the same direction for very long after the end of the GEW. Rivalries between Italy and Turkey in the Eastern Mediterranean and North Africa on the one hand, and between Italy and Austria-Hungary in the Tyrol and on the Adriatic on the other hand, practically guaranteed future conflicts and an early end to the German alliance system. A brief summary of those rivalries makes this point clear.

The Ottoman Empire and the Kingdom of Italy fought the Tripolitanian War from September 29, 1911 to October 18, 1912. Victorious Italy seized the Turkish North African provinces of Tripolitania, Fezzan, and Cyrenaica, forming the colony of Libya. It is likely that the Ottoman Empire, had it survived the war, would have made some effort to recover these lost provinces.

Italy had a long history of conflict with the Austro-Hungarian Empire prior to 1914. Indeed, the birth of an independent nation of Italy came only after three wars of independence against the Dual Monarchy. Even after the Kingdom of Italy was established in 1871, Austria still retained territory claimed by Italy. This *terre irredente* in the Alps and along the Adriatic coast was Italy's reward for its joining the Entente in 1915. In WWI, Italy suffered more than 600,000 killed and nearly 1 million wounded during offensives against Austria, trying to take the *irredente*. In light of this, it is difficult to see how Germany could have kept these two nations on the same team for very long, as Italy was unlikely to forego permanently its demands for these "lost" territories, and Austria-Hungary was equally unlikely to concede them without a war.

WWI did not merely affect international politics; it was the direct cause of great changes in the very structure of society. In four years of total national mobilization, all the combatant countries were forced to staff their factories with women while the men were away in the trenches. This was the first time in history that the female populations of Western nations were called upon to provide the majority of the labor force. In Great Britain, by 1917 there were 819,000 women working in the munitions industry alone. In France at the war's end, 425,000 women were working in state-run armaments factories, with a further 132,000 in the privately owned metal industry compared with only 17,731 at the start of the war.

WWI dramatically expanded the role of the state in daily life, as it took over direction of the economies of the contending nations, imposing cooperation on capital and labor to support the demands of the military machines. By 1918, General Erich Ludendorff was in an unprecedented position as virtual dictator of Germany, having assumed direction of practically every aspect of the economy, in addition to his control of the army. The scope of governments in France and Britain had also grown tremendously. This growth would prove, after the war, to be the first step in the growth of the modern social welfare state. Whether these profound changes would have occurred anyway is impossible to say, but it is certain that it would not have happened so quickly without the pressure of four years of total war.

I will not speculate to what extent the second great trauma of the 20th Century, the Great Depression, would have been affected by the relatively short and inexpensive GEW. There are too many conflicting views among historians and economists about the relationship between WWI and the Depression. Some scholars believe WWI was the principal cause of the Depression, or one of the principal causes. Some hold that it was one cause among many, and yet others that the two events had no causal relationship at all. Under the circumstances, I will only say that there must have been *some* substantial long term consequences arising from the unprecedented disruptions of the participants' economies in WWI, and that this had an effect on the size and possibly the timing of the Great Depression. Whatever that effect was, obviously it would not have been a consequence of the GEW.

Afterword Three:
Aeroplanes, Tanks, and Other Toys: Technology and the Great War

World War One was the first modern war where the contestants organized their entire industrial outputs for war. It was only by this total mobilization of labor, capital and national resources that Great Britain, France, Germany and Austria-Hungary were able to raise and equip armies of millions of men, supply them with what they needed to fight: weapons, ammunition, transport, food and so forth; and keep them supplied for a war lasting four long years.

It is practically a truism that modern war accelerates technological innovation. In WWI, the technology of the machine gun and quick-firing artillery, combined with barbed wire, created a deadlock on the Western Front. The only solution the commanding generals had to offer was to hurl the unprotected bodies of their men at entrenched machine guns. Military technology had created conditions which made offensive warfare too expensive in lives to be practical. This was obviously unsatisfactory. How could the war ever be won if neither side was able to successfully attack the other?

But a stalemate created by machines could be broken by other machines. If the attackers could bring their firepower with them, to use while they were protected from enemy machine guns, perhaps progress could be made at a bearable price in casualties. This line of thinking resulted in the birth of the tank. This weapons system combined the comparatively new technology of the internal combustion engine with the ancient one of armor. The tank was introduced by the British in 1916, at the Battle of the Somme. The engines of the day were just barely powerful enough to move the machines at all (top speed: 4 miles per hour), and they were so unreliable that many of them broke down before reaching the start line. Even so, it was clear by the end of the war that this new weapon had the potential to restore movement to warfare.

In the GEW, there was no massive deadlock on the Western Front comparable to the one in 1914-1918. Moreover, Great Britain remained neutral throughout. So, the tank would not have been invented, not in 1916, at any rate. But, would it ever have been invented?

I feel quite confident in answering "yes". A steam-powered log-hauler with a type of continuous or "caterpillar" track was in service by 1901, and caterpillar tractors with internal combustion engines were being manufactured by 1907. The armored car, mounting a machine gun and powered by a gasoline engine, made its debut as early as 1902, and was used by both sides in 1914. (see the article "Armored Cars" by David Zabecki in: *An Encyclopedia of World War One* (1999), Spencer Tucker, *ed.*) Thus, all the components of the tank were already at hand before 1914: it merely required the imagination to put the pieces together to create a practical weapon and the financing to pay for its development. Still, the birth of the tank would probably have been delayed until the next Great Power war after the GEW, as few governments (especially the U.S. and Great Britain) would be willing to spend the necessary funds on experimental weapons in peacetime

Another technology whose development was greatly accelerated by WWI was heavier-than-air flight, i.e., the airplane. Stephan Fejes' Lohner B. VI reconnaissance plane, with its top speed of 115 kph, was the state of the art in 1914. But the pressure of the ongoing war soon made such aircraft obsolete, especially on the Western Front. The most important advances in aircraft technology were the introduction of new, more powerful engines and the construction of stronger, lighter and more aerodynamically-efficient airframes.

224

For example, the British started the war with the B.E. 2 Scout, powered by a 90 hp RAF 1a. engine which gave it performance characteristics very similar to that of the Lohner (maximum speed: 116 kilometers per hour, service ceiling: 3050 meters). But by 1917, Royal Flying Corps (predecessor to the RAF) had airplanes that made the B.E. 2 look as if they had been built in a previous century. For example, the Bristol Fighter boasted a 270 hp Rolls Royce Falcon III engine with a top speed of 198 kph and a ceiling of 6500 m.

Not only did the war inspire the production of faster planes, it also led to the invention of aerial bombing and the development of machines with far greater payloads than anyone but the most visionary air enthusiast in 1914 could have imagined. The Handley-Page V/1500, powered by four 375 hp Roll-Royce engines, had a bomb capacity of 7500 pounds. This plane and others like it demonstrated the commercial possibilities of heavier-than-air aviation, which boomed in the inter-war period. The first commercial airline was started immediately after the war, in 1919, using converted Handley Page bombers to fly the London-Paris route. By 1935, Pan-American World Airways was offering air service from the United States to South America, Europe and the Pacific aboard their huge Sikorsky flying boats, and Imperial Airways had established an air route from London to Egypt, India and eventually Australia, linking the far-flung British Empire by air. The V/1500 was also the first in a long line of strategic bombers, like the Avro Lancaster and the B-17 Flying Fortress of WWII, which demonstrated the destructive potential of airpower, erasing entire cities from the map in thousand-plane raids and adding a new, terrifying word to the English language: "firestorm".

Aviation, both commercial and military, made huge strides in the inter-war years, so that by 1939, modern all-metal monoplanes were capable of speeds, payloads and ranges un-dreamt of in the previous war. But none this progress could have been made without the innovations brought about by the pressures of total war from 1914 to 1918. It is impossible to say even approximately when these developments would have occurred if WWI had not happened, but it is certain that the progress of military aviation would have been retarded for decades at the very least.

The effect of the GEW on the development of the system that revolutionized warfare in 1939, "lightning war" or "blitzkrieg", would have been profound. Lightning war, as practiced by the Germans, who were the first to make the combination work, involved the use of massed armored vehicles in cooperation with tactical aircraft. The armored spearheads were designed to break through the enemy lines at a key point, (the "schwerpunkt") and drive deep into his rear areas, destroying the defender's communications, supply lines and basic cohesion. The tanks were followed by masses of motorized infantry and artillery, which would pour through the gap in an "expanding torrent". Much of the necessary groundwork to make the concept a reality was done in the Britain during the 1920s by the Experimental Mechanized Force under the leadership of J.F.C. Fuller, including the use of radios to control the tank force, and the development of self-propelled artillery and tracked troop carriers capable of following the armor off the roads to exploit breakthroughs.

Without the great advances in aviation along with the invention and development of the tank in WWI, none of which would have occurred in the GEW, the basis for this new form of warfare would not have existed at all. It is quite likely, indeed probable, that the next Great Power war after the GEW would have been fought, at the beginning at least, with weapons and tactics very much like those of the previous conflict.

In Conclusion

What if anything, can be learned from this counterfactual examination of the Schlieffen Plan? I would argue that it stands as a case study and a warning to policy makers as an example of the potentially disastrous consequences that can follow when political leaders, such as Wilhelm II, abdicate their responsibilities by leaving political/diplomatic decisions to their generals. Had its political leadership acted responsibly, Germany would have been spared the consequences of defeat after four years of bloody warfare, and the rest of the world the convulsion of 1939-1945 that resulted from that defeat.

Andrew J Heller
Erdenheim, PA

Made in the USA
Columbia, SC
29 January 2022

54998781R00138